To Lyndsey

The

I hope you enjoy the read.
Your mum tells me it's
your birthday, so...
HAPPY BIRTHDAY!!!

J. MEDLAND

THE MOORS

First published in July 2015 by
Pen Works Media Ltd
1 Yasmin James Villas, London, N11 2LP

This book is a work of fiction.

www.penworksmedia.co.uk

Printed in England by Clays Ltd, St Ives plc

ISBN: 978-1-908730-14-5

"Three may keep a secret, if two of them are dead."
Benjamin Franklin

Contents

Prologue

BEING ABUSED AS A CHILD appeared to be the most common factor when analysing the backgrounds of rapists and serial killers, but this was something Amanda Connors never fully understood.

When she was a girl, her stepfather took liberties no adult ever should with a child. He did it not once, but on a regular basis for a period of almost three years. It was a phase of her life that certainly shaped her, but she was determined not to let such ill-treatment define her. She was tired of seeing people spend their lives blaming their problems on things that happened in the past and using them as an excuse not to create a brighter future.

This would never be her.

She would not be a victim.

Stored away somewhere in a dark corner of her mind was a series of hidden memories, buried in a place no person would think to look.

The house Amanda grew up in was somewhat pokey. Islington was full of such buildings that had families and their belongings spilling out onto their lawns, but in general the people of North London had a certain ability to carry on even when things got tough.

Bright red. That was the colour of the door at Amanda's modest house, which always stuck in the frame as her abuser fumbled at it when drunk. A weak push, as if forgetting the door was ill-fitting, was followed by a second sturdier effort that still wasn't enough to force the door open. There would be a momentary silence, as though he needed to study the problem, before an overtly powerful shove overcame the obstacle with ease. He would then close the door so hard that it shook the walls throughout the entire house.

At this point, Amanda would close her eyes and pretend she was asleep, a peculiar habit as it never stopped him taking what he wanted. She would lie in silence as his feet clumsily staggered up the stairs, his body landing against the wall as he continually fought for balance. She often prayed he would slip and fall back down, but he never did. She equated hearing him struggling up the stairs to feeling sick. There was nothing worse than feeling her cheeks tingle and her brow and palms grow clammy as nausea took a hold of her and she knew she was about to vomit.

Well… almost nothing worse.

On occasion, he would walk right past Amanda's room and pester her mother, who he rarely assaulted sexually. He was violent towards her in other ways and listening to the beatings was a very different kind of helplessness.

On the rare occasion he would be so completely inebriated that he would just fall onto one of their beds and pass out.

Those were the good days.

As he lingered at the top of the staircase, his shadow could be seen interrupting the soft orange glow that crept underneath Amanda's door from the hallway. She would sometimes stare at the swaying shadow, willing it away as her heart pounded against her chest. She would always know when her luck was out. The cheap metal doorknob would squeak as he twisted it in his hand. The latch would make the noise of a winding spring as it retracted, allowing him to stumble through the doorway. The naked floorboards would creak and the unwelcome scent of smoke and ale would infiltrate her room. It was an odour that always made her grimace.

As he inched towards her bed, she would hear a series of lazy unfastening and unzipping sounds and when he was close enough, his perverted wheezy breath would rise and fall as he looked down over her body. He would run his grubby, smoky fingers through her hair, making her skin crawl and her eyes close still tighter as she attempted to reject what was happening. By the time he would clamber onto her bed – always leading with his knee and causing the springs to scream weakly, as though calling for help they knew would never come – Amanda had invariably found her "safe place." It was this magical haven that spared her from further details of these endless encounters. The next thing she knew, she would look up to see him slumped over her, crying as he begged for forgiveness. Even at her tender age and vulnerable proximity, she found it a pathetic sight, mainly because she knew he would not have the power to keep the promises he made – neither to her or himself.

This would never be her.
She would not be a victim.

It would have been all too easy for Amanda to blame her problems on the countless nights that stole her innocence. It would have been just as easy to feel bitterness towards a youth that had been so heavily stained. However, this simply wasn't who Amanda was.

She could not support the argument that abuse was a by-product of earlier abuse and that it was an unbreakable cycle. Instead, she condemned anybody who used such stories as some form of defence for doing wrong towards others. In her experience, the fact she had been handled so neglectfully made her *more* determined to treat people well. It made her *more* motivated to keep people – particularly children – safe, so they did not have to suffer the same misfortunes she did.

In a twisted form of logic, Amanda embraced what had happened to her. It had made her a better person, more grounded and aware.

Her stepfather died young of Crohn's disease, an illness that had plagued him from birth and had robbed him of his younger years. Incredibly, she was able to feel pity for him and reasoned that his actions probably stemmed from not being able to experience "normal" interactions with girls during his adolescence. Did that make it right? Of course not, but at least it provided some kind of explanation for his behaviour, allowing her to put the events in a box that she could store away.

As it was, the one person Amanda was never able to forgive was her mother, who sat by and allowed the abuse to take place. Not once did she validate Amanda's stories about what was happening and she even punished Amanda for speaking up. Now that Amanda was older, she could tell her mother knew he was guilty, yet denying the reality was simply more convenient. To Amanda, denial was the highest form of weakness and was a trait she had grown to loathe. Every time the front door closed in that house, Amanda – a young, helpless girl – knew exactly what to expect, so it simply wasn't feasible for her mother to be lying in bed oblivious in the very next room. No. She *must* have been aware and could have stopped it at any moment. Instead, she turned a blind eye, and that was simply unforgivable.

This would never be her.
She would not be a victim.

After a few years of working in care, Amanda realised it was a deeply rewarding career but one that came with many limits. Therefore, she combined her desire to help those in need with her ability to write in the most beautifully expressive way. It was in her early twenties that she discovered the power of journalism. It gave her a voice with which to speak and, more importantly, a platform where people would listen. Her curious nature led her to many great stories and it wasn't long before she had carved out a reputation as a fearless investigatory journalist. Her work was so good, in fact, that she won a position at *The Times* when women were considered far from equal. Her brief was to generate the type of hard-hitting material that would give the paper an edge over their competitors, and she certainly achieved that.

In the winter of 1972, whilst sitting in the editorial office, she received an anonymous phone call. Distressed, the caller sobbed down the phone saying they had been to the Prince Care Home and had witnessed something truly horrible. The call was brief but prominent and by the time the line went dead, Amanda's research had already begun.

The Prince Care Home was based in the middle of Exmoor in North Devon and had housed both physically and mentally ill children since 1960. The property was owned and managed by one Christian Prince, who had recently started advertising for a carer. Without a second thought, Amanda applied for the job and after a successful telephone interview, she was hired.

Suddenly, Amanda felt vindicated, as though every single event that had unfolded in her life had led her to that moment for a reason and handed her a story that was surely her destiny.

As she boarded the First Great Western train from London Paddington to Tiverton Parkway, she felt as though an inexplicable force was guiding her. Its power was so great that all she could do was allow herself to follow. After all, following her instincts had always stood her in good stead before.

She looked out of the window as the large buildings of the city fell away, replaced by fields and greenery that held a different kind of beauty. The closer she came to her destination, the greater the adrenalin that rushed through her veins.

She busied herself by reading the morning papers. On every page, another horror story: a baby found dead in a bin, a wife stabbed by her husband in a jealous rage, a man beaten to death for being gay. She spared a thought for each of the victims before repeating the mantra that had seen her transform herself from an unfortunate child into a strong and powerful woman.

This will never be me.

I will not be a victim.

Suddenly, the train slowed to a gradual halt and there, outside of Amanda's window, was a tall, rusty sign that read: *Tiverton Parkway*.

She had arrived, and this is where the grisly story begins.

The Moors

Some secrets are better left buried

CHAPTER ONE

The Station Call

Friday 11th February, 1972

Sometimes when landing upon a new place, a person can get a good sense of what to expect almost immediately. Amanda had never been to the West Country before. Her first impressions of Devon were surprising, but not at all complimentary. Something about the manner of the roadside café where an elderly waitress glared at her whilst pouring coffee for a truck driver reeked of outback America. Amanda felt uncomfortable from the moment she stepped onto the rickety old platform, but then again, she seldom felt comfortable anywhere outside of the city. Her mind was quick, some might say manic, and when the surroundings didn't match her inner intensity, it often caused her to become restless.

Amanda's piercing green eyes hinted at a beauty often buried beneath expensive suits and a moody yet focused expression, which she displayed as she juggled multiple sugar sachets above a polystyrene cup whilst speaking quietly into a payphone.

'It was okay. The train pulled in early if you can believe—'

An unexpected tear in the sachet sprayed white grains of sugar everywhere.

'Shit!' she cursed, attracting unwanted attention.

'What's wr—g?' asked a male voice on the other end of the line, the phone crackling as he did so.

'What?' asked Amanda, frowning as she pressed her ear hard against the earpiece.

'What's wrong?' the man repeated, this time clearly, as Amanda fussed over the mess she'd made.

'Sorry. The line's pretty bad. Nothing's wrong. I'm fine,' she said, quickly realising Tony would decipher her lie.

She tried to coax the sugar into a napkin, but to no avail. Disapproving looks from the locals were met with a defiant glare of her own.

City mouse was in no mood to play.

'I wish I could believe it,' said Tony.

'Fine! Everything. Everything's wrong!' she snapped. 'Tony, I...'

'Hey! It's okay. We'll b- -kay,' he insisted.

She imagined the expression on his face; the prominent wrinkle that appeared in the middle of his forehead whenever he spoke delicately and the look of sincerity that was ever present in his deep brown trustworthy eyes. These were the traits that first endeared him to Amanda. She was not the type of person to hand out her trust freely. She didn't often make friends as, when it came down to it, she saw friendship as an inconvenience that sapped her time and energy – two invaluable assets that were better spent on pursuing her career. She was even more selective when it came to potential lovers.

Tony was her senior editor and because of this, they spent countless hours together. Had that not been the case, their friendship would have been unlikely to grow. However, the passion they shared for their profession provided them with a common ground on which their bond could flourish. With Tony, she never had to apologise for her unpredictable schedule. Unlike most men who were intimidated by her ambition, he was very much an advocate of it. What's more, he fully respected her boundaries and never repeated questions that she seemed reluctant to answer.

These were the many factors necessary for Amanda to consider falling in love, but love was hard and just recently Tony had asked for her hand in marriage. When she questioned his reasons, he told her straight. He longed for a future where they would live together, share a bank account, plan their movements around one another and begin a family, linking them for the rest of their lives. It was all too much for Amanda to comprehend. Sure, she could see the validity in why he might view such things as progress in their relationship, but she was reluctant to bring a child into a world as vile as the one that surrounded them.

This was a difference in opinion that was sure to prove a major problem. There was simply no denying it.

Amanda rested her head against the payphone, looking more regretful than consoled.

'You'll be back in three days,' Tony reminded her. 'We can talk then.'

The fact he had been so lovely, caring only about her feelings and forfeiting that of his own, only served to make her feel worse.

She wished she had not left on such bad terms.

'I guess,' she said, resigned to the fact she had no other option.

'And that's *three* days. You'll be back here on Sunday, as agreed. Okay?' said Tony.

'Yeah,' she agreed, softly.

'Because I know what you're like when you get your teeth into something and if you try to go back on your word, I'll come down there and pull you out myself!' he continued, in a mini-rant that was heavily based on past experience.

Amanda smiled, her spirit lifted.

'Yes, boss! Message received,' she replied, playfully.

'I do l--- you,' he said, the interference cheating Amanda of the word she most needed to hear.

'You too,' she replied, before placing the phone back onto the receiver.

She took a moment to collect her thoughts and then picked up her suitcase.

'You gonna clean that up?' asked the waitress, the positioning of her chubby arms making her look like a short, dumpy teapot.

'No. You are,' stated Amanda, before striding across the floor donning a superior posture.

'Oooooooh...' goaded the truck driver, causing the waitress to snatch his mug away.

'Hey! I'm not done,' he grumbled.

'Yes you are,' the waitress scorned.

*

Amanda grimaced at the stench of stale urine in the ladies' toilets. Ordinarily, she wouldn't have accepted such standards but as far as she could see these were the only facilities for miles around. Besides, her ride was soon to arrive, giving her little time to be fussy.

She placed her suitcase on the floor and squinted to see her reflection in the grimy mirror. She attempted to run some cold water from the tap but the banging pipes only offered spurts of brown liquid. She turned the tap off immediately and recoiled, pulling on a fresh top and placing a black hairband over her soft shoulder-length hair with precision. It was amazing how those two simple items combined with her fake but brilliant smile to make her appear so much younger than her thirty-one years. The face that now looked back was not Amanda Connors but Amanda Green – the innocent yet inquisitive alter-ego she'd created for the job. The character was well rehearsed and gave her the greatest chance of extracting the most information whilst remaining unobtrusive. As she stepped out of the dingy bathroom, she was ready to implement the first phase of her plan.

*

Within the classic frame of a black BMW, Amanda stole subtle glances of Walter – a tall, skinny man with a calm and quiet manner. His white hair thinned at the top of his head and his temples pulsed as he took great pleasure in sucking on a sweet.

'Nervous?' he asked, taking her quite by surprise.

The quiet ones were always the most observant, but she was able to pass off her obvious tension by assuming the role of her wide-eyed, desperately naive pseudonym.

'Oh! No. I was just admiring the view. It's beautiful around here,' she gushed. 'Much greener than the city.'

She watched Walter out the corner of her eye as he drove. Each movement was meticulous and assured. Every word he spoke had purpose.

'You know what? Maybe I am a little nervous!' she said as she squeezed her palms, curious to discover how he would respond to small talk.

'Don't be. You'll settle,' he assured her.

He was polite, but already his short answers suggested he didn't particularly enjoy questions, which prompted her to ask more.

'On the phone, Christian said you used to be a butler?' she asked.

'Yes. It was some time ago but it's rather ingrained into me, I'm afraid. Even now, I find certain habits difficult to drop!' he said, shifting in his seat and smiling as though he had been tickled.

'And now you're a carer?'

'In a way. I live in the home with my wife,' he replied.

'Your wife?' queried Amanda.

He nodded.

'Yes dear. Christian is our son-in-law.'

Amanda fell silent for a moment.

So there are two families that run the home.

'Wouldn't you rather retire somewhere other than a care home?' she asked, quite abruptly.

To this question, Walter became somewhat guarded, as he had been before humour momentarily breached his defences. She noticed him grip the steering wheel as he chose his words carefully.

'It's a long story,' came his eventual response, before he pulled a small white paper bag out of his pocket, waving it in front of her.

'Would you like a sweet?' he asked as part of a clear diversion tactic.

Amanda glanced inside the bag to see a huddle of claret aniseed balls.

'No. Thank you,' she replied.

Walter shrugged before popping one into his mouth, providing him with yet another perfect excuse not to talk.

Very cunning! She thought.

In the silence, Amanda paid more attention to her surroundings. From Tiverton Parkway rail station, they had travelled through small link roads and endless winding country lanes. Only a couple of incredibly small towns showed any signs of normality before a road sign welcomed them to Exmoor.

Amanda suddenly became aware that they were completely alone and even the roads disappeared into nothing more than a dirt track that led them to two very tall, impossibly heavy-looking iron gates. They were the kind clearly meant to stop intruders, but as Amanda looked around, she wondered who on earth might be passing by.

Walter stepped out of the car and flicked through a number of keys before unlocking a thick metal chain, which was wrapped around the gates like a snake squeezing the life from its prey. As he walked back to the car, she wondered if the gates were in fact more for keeping people in than out.

She absorbed the landscape. Visually, the place was utterly stunning. Freshly cut grass and healthy green trees separated a number of clearly defined gardens and a seating area. Endless flowers offered sharp injections of colour that really brightened up the place and a quaint pond sat beside the dirt track on which they drove. At the top of the hill, which was much longer than Amanda first thought, an old three storey building appeared from behind the trees, emerging as if by magic and standing in proud isolation, watching over the land like a lighthouse in the middle of the sea. The building was majestic, dauntingly so.

The car park, which offered an impressive number of spaces, had only one other vehicle in it. Due to Amanda's lack of automotive knowledge she could only surmise it as a shiny jeep. Amanda sensed it was expensive, but the fact it reminded her of a hearse limited the vehicle's charm. Walter parked and without saying a word headed for the back of the car to retrieve Amanda's suitcase. He was right. Being a butler had become part of his DNA.

Amanda could normally gauge people within two minutes of meeting them. It was one of her party tricks and a useful ability to have in her line of work, but Walter was interesting; harder to read than most. He appeared to be a traditional gentleman who kept the majority of his thoughts to himself. He possessed loyalty and kindness yet held an element of mystery, which Amanda found a rare and admirable combination. She looked towards the house with purpose, noticing something in an upstairs window. It was the pale old face of a woman who soon stepped out of view.

Amanda's concentration was broken as Walter slammed the boot shut and stepped towards her, bag-in-hand.

'Ready?' he asked, possessing the slightest hint of a smile.

She was.

She had been for years, and if there was anything amiss within the home, she intended to bring the whole place down, brick-by-brick.

CHAPTER TWO

The Help

Friday 11th February, 1972

As a fan of classic literature, Amanda couldn't help but find comparisons between her entry into the home to Jonathan Harker's first visit to Count Dracula's castle. Everything that unfolded around her could have been interpreted as creepy – from the backward people in the roadside café and the ghostly face in the window to the way the key clunked heavily in the lock. The door squeaked somewhat eerily as Walter pushed it open. Even Walter, the man she had so warmed to, suddenly bared a remarkable resemblance to the Count himself, with his tall, thin frame, pale skin and crooked smile now appearing rather sinister since being placed in a gothic surrounding.

This was the most problematic part of being an investigatory journalist. By Amanda's very nature, she was led by curiosity and intrigue, meaning there was always a danger she would manifest fictitious realities. This had happened once before when she harmed the reputation of a businessman who turned out to be innocent, believing he had made his money through unlawful means by using a dry-cleaning business to launder money. In fairness, the man in question had a very public and unsavoury background as a gangster, so the fact the propaganda and slander caused by Amanda's articles put his business under was seen by many as a good dose of karma, though not by Amanda herself. She wanted to catch wrongdoers and expose them more than anything, but as a woman of integrity, she wished to do things the right way. Also, had it not been for the full support of Tony, she would have almost certainly lost her job and she shuddered to think what life would be like without journalism.

People in her profession walked a very thin tightrope indeed. Without having the guts to pursue leads in the first place, justice would seldom be given the opportunity to prevail, but if they pushed things just a little too far, their reputations and careers were likely to be left in tatters. It never stopped Amanda snooping, though. In many ways, she was fearless. There were times when she hoped her instincts were wrong though, and her visit to Exmoor was such an occasion. She would much prefer to waste a few days' work over a prank call than discover the children were the subject of abuse. To uncover such stories was an exhausting process for everybody involved and she already felt as though she was running on empty. When she had awoken that morning, she had a deep sickly feeling in her belly. It could have been caused by a number of reasons: the distress she felt over her recent fallout with Tony, the fact she was about to tackle a potentially significant story or simply because her body was willing her to slow down.

As Amanda stepped through the front door, something within her changed. Like a boxer stepping into the ring, absorbing the crowd and breathing in the atmosphere, her nose twitched as she sized up her surroundings. One of the things she most loved about her job was that it afforded her the luxury of forgetting everything else. Quite simply, the real world ceased to exist until her work was done and now that she had reached the location, she had no intention of leaving the building until she knew exactly what went on between the four tall and sturdy walls that encompassed her. She needed to remain level headed but suspicious. That was the only way to uncover truth without bias.

The corridor was long and led to a grand staircase. An opening to her right invited her into a large, plush drawing room. Midway down the corridor another hallway shot off to the left. Abstract paintings hung from the walls and expensive looking ornaments filled the shelves. Only one thing was abundantly clear – this home could not have been created without a significant injection of money.

A gold plaque screwed onto the wall read:

The Prince Care Home
Est. 1960

Amanda took mental pictures of everything around her: the cleanliness of the halls, the exceptionally high ceilings and the large rooms.

'I'm not quite sure where everybody is,' stated Walter. 'Let me find Margaret. She'll show you around. Please… make yourself at home.'

Amanda watched him carry her suitcase down the hall and as he made his way up the stairs she stepped rather inquisitively into the drawing room. Two large windows allowed the light to pour inside. Amanda's intention was to nose around for objects of interest, but instead, she froze. She could hear irregular breathing – it was slight but sure – and beneath one of the large, heavy curtains that draped down the side of the living room window stood two small feet. Amanda looked around. She was utterly alone. Nobody was in sight and there was no other sound... except for that which came from behind the curtain. Slowly and cautiously, she approached. The breathing became heavier and more infrequent as she inched forward and reached out her hand. She envisaged pulling back the curtain to reveal some kind of freakish being; a monster that would be more at home in a nineteenth century travelling fair than stood in a children's care home. She willed her imagination to calm down when a frightened whisper came from behind her.

'There's somebody else in the room,' said the voice.

Amanda's head whipped around to see a young girl staring directly at her, though her eyes were white pigment.

*

Amanda's screams travelled through the halls like some kind of evil spirit warning its inhabitants of a bygone misery. Margaret – a jolly old tubby woman born and bred in the West Country – was changing bed sheets when they finally reached her. In many ways, Margaret was the life and soul of the home; a fixer of sorts, and her reaction was one of habit as she rolled her eyes and headed towards the door.

'Hang on. I'm coming!' she yelled in her strong yet soothing accent.

By the time she reached the lounge, Georgina Smith – the blind nine-year-old who had given Amanda such a fright – was the one screaming. Still behind the curtain was twelve-year-old Reuben Thomas – a wavy haired boy who spoke with a stutter. He covered his ears and rocked nervously back and forth, wishing the noises away.

'No. It's okay! I'm sorry,' insisted Amanda, who was trying her best to calm the girl down.

Margaret entered the room and placed a tender hand on Georgina's shoulder, gently squeezing her in just the right way before affectionately running her fingers through the girl's hair.

'Georgie, my love. What's all the fuss about?' she soothed. 'It's alright.'

Finally, the screams disappeared and the sound of Margaret's voice brought Reuben out from behind the curtain. He ran behind Margaret and used her as a protective shield as he stole curious glimpses of the stranger.

Amanda recognised Margaret. The woman had once taken care of her in a care home called Saint Matthews. At the time, she was going through something of a rebellious stage, only wearing black clothes and eye shadow as she worked through a host of internal issues. She desperately hoped Margaret wouldn't connect the stroppy, black-haired teenager to the woman she had become.

'I'm so sorry,' apologised Amanda.

'No-no. It's alright,' Margaret assured her. 'You shouldn't have been left alone. I didn't hear you come in, that's all. Kids, this is Amanda. She's come to help us look after you. That'll be nice, won't it?'

Margaret's voice was full of encouragement, but the children seemed uncertain.

'Amanda, this is Reuben and Georgina.'

Amanda painted on her best smile.

'Both wonderful names!' she gushed.

Without warning, Margaret turned her head and yelled out into the corridor.

'Christian? Christian!' she shouted.

'What?' asked a pre-occupied voice from an unknown crevice of the house.

'Don't yell. Get in here! I didn't raise you to be lazy!'

Christian's mother. Amanda noted.

'Ha! He hates it when I say that, doesn't he?' Margaret said to the children, who chuckled in delight.

Indeed, her personality was so infectious that even Amanda's lips broke into a crescent of a smile.

20

Christian emerged in the middle of a complaint as he wiped what looked like oil from his forearm.

'I'm not the one who was…'

Upon seeing Amanda, his posture became immdediately more authoritative.

'Hi!' was the greeting he eventually pushed out.

'Hello,' she replied, accompanied with the kind of smile that very few men would be able to resist.

'This is Amanda,' chimed Margaret.

'I know who she is, Mother!' he scoffed.

As a people-watcher, Amanda always found it amusing that no matter how old a person became, their mannerisms and expressions often reverted back to childhood when talking to a parent.

'If you're gonna be stroppy you should go to bed earlier,' teased Margaret, further supporting Amanda's observation. 'He's not too old for a smacked bum, is he?' Margaret asked the children.

They both giggled as Margaret guided them towards Christian.

'I need you to keep these two out of trouble while I show Amanda to her room. Think you can manage that?' she jested.

'Oh! I don't know,' responded Christian, who had finally given up resisting his mother's banter. 'They'll probably get bored. I was just going to get some ice-cream.'

'I like ice-cream,' Georgina informed him in a stroppy tone.

'You do?' asked Christian as he feigned surprise.

'Yah! That's not boring!' insisted Reuben.

'Well in that case, I guess you better come with me!' he enthused.

'Don't give them too much or you'll spoil their appetite,' said Margaret.

'No he won't,' claimed Georgina, rather feebly.

'Oh yeah? We'll see if you're as optimistic when I ask you to eat your greens later!'

'What are greens?' she asked.

'Vegetables,' Margaret replied.

Georgina immediately screwed up her face.

'That's what I thought,' said Margaret as she rolled her eyes at Amanda. 'But if you don't promise to eat them, no ice-cream!'

'Isn't that blackmail?' questioned Georgina.

'Call it what you want!' said Margaret, unaffected, as she ushered them out of the room.

'It was nice to meet you,' called Amanda, her eyes locked on Christian, who smiled before leading the children away through the dining room, which also led out into the kitchen. Amanda noticed Reuben whispering something into Georgina's ear, which made her stare directly back at Amanda. Something about those plain white eyes sent a shiver down her spine.

'Come on, my love,' said Margaret, interrupting Amanda's thoughts as she coaxed her away.

Amanda keenly observed the layout of the house as Margaret led her through the downstairs hallway.

'Living room, dining room, kitchen,' Margaret said, pointing to her right. 'Christian's office, Christian's bedroom, Malcolm's bedroom,' she continued, pointing to her left. 'Malcolm's the only one of our children who sleeps downstairs. The rest are up on the first floor with us. Underneath the stairs is where we keep the children's toys and right here is the communal toilet and bathroom. It's the only one we have, I'm afraid,' she confirmed as she led Amanda upstairs.

The house was somehow even bigger than it seemed from the outside. The walls were painted in warm colours – rich oranges and reds, with large candle holders lined neatly along each wall.

'Amanda Green...' said Margaret aloud. 'I don't recognise the name but you seem awfully familiar. Might I know you from somewhere?'

'I don't think so,' dismissed Amanda.

Upon reaching the first floor, Amanda observed that there were four rooms to her left and three to her right, with another hallway branching off to the right at the end of the corridor. Only some of the doors were numbered – 2 and 3 labelled the two middle doors on her left with 4 and 5 marking the adjacent rooms to her right. Amanda noted how different the place felt compared to the ground floor. The décor was the same but it felt darker, colder and much less homely. The ceilings appeared lower in the hallway and the seven doorways in view made the space appear more congested. Without any explanation regarding the layout,

Margaret led Amanda straight towards the first room on their left and pushed the door open.

'This is where you'll be staying,' she said, wearing a grin as she stood aside invitingly.

As Amanda entered she saw that her suitcase had been placed at the foot of the large double bed that lay in wait for her. She inadvertently twirled around as she absorbed the room. It appeared freshly decorated with vibrant colours that enriched her mood. She had a generously sized wardrobe and an elegant dresser that sat underneath a large window, offering a picturesque view of the moors. A beautiful blue lake lay in the distance. Suddenly, Amanda slipped into her dumfounded persona a little too easily, bewitched by the efforts they had made for her. As she looked back to Margaret, who keenly observed her reaction, she fought to contain the little girl inside of her who wanted to burst in delight. Instead, she simply nodded in approval.

'It's much bigger than I expected,' was the understated response she allowed to pass her lips.

It was still enough to make Margaret smile proudly.

'You like it?' she pressed.

'Very much,' Amanda assured her.

'Good. I'm glad,' said Margaret, her happiness clear.

It was almost impossible to spend time with Margaret without wanting to hug her.

If only all mothers were like this. Amanda secretly contemplated.

'I'm gonna let you get settled. You'll probably want to get some rest,' presumed Margaret.

'Thank you, Margaret,' said Amanda, from a much deeper place than the woman could have known.

'Maggie. Please,' she replied, letting the new recruit know she was already considered a friend.

Amanda nodded and looked at the woman, this vibrant woman whose love and affection was so clear, as it had been many years earlier. This was not the kind of person Amanda had expected to find and as Margaret quietly disappeared into the hallway, Amanda hoped the others would be just like her.

CHAPTER THREE

The Story Begins

Friday 11th February, 1972

Amanda wasted no time before examining the nooks and crannies of the room. Her movements were rather militant as she explored the wardrobe. She found a portable radio that had been placed out of the way on the top shelf. It was old and a thick layer of dust suggested it had been there for some time, probably forgotten about entirely. Other than that and a selection of clothes hangers, the wardrobe was completely bare. Amanda reasoned that Margaret had cleared it for their arrival and probably failed to detect the radio as it was stored right at the back. Even she needed to stand on a chair to find it and she had a considerable height advantage.

On the bed, Amanda opened her suitcase, removing a stack of neatly folded clothes to reveal a cluster of notebooks, pens and non-fiction books on Exmoor and various mental illnesses. She glided across the floor, climbed back on the chair and placed the items in her new secret hiding place. She walked back to her suitcase and from a special compartment hidden within its lining pulled out a small silver Dictaphone, perfect for recording short, sharp statements whilst they were still fresh in her mind. She considered the record button before looking ponderously towards the bedroom door. A quick glance into the first floor hallway revealed that nobody was in sight, but she was new to the house and therefore unsure of how far her voice might travel. Amanda took no chances and placed the radio on the dresser. She switched it on and adjusted the volume until satisfied it would distort her voice to any passers-by. Finally, she pressed record on her device and held it close to her mouth as she spoke under her breath.

'Amanda Connors. Day one,' she began.

Everything about her changed when she entered work mode. She was always thinking, obsessive about details. Her tone was serious, as was the look on her face. She was a completely different person to the Amanda that the home's occupants would get to meet.

'I've just arrived at the residence. Initial meetings have been held with carers Walter Ambrose, Margaret Prince and Christian Prince. I've met Margaret before but she doesn't remember me. She cared for me at Saint Matthews when I was young. I've also met residents Reuben and Georgina. Not much else to report so far. They've all been kind. Margaret, in particular, seems to have a special bond with the children, who suffer from more severe conditions than I'd anticipated. More to follow when I meet the others.'

She clicked stop and closed her eyes, slowly rotating her head as she massaged the knots in her neck. Not until that moment had she absorbed the commentary on the radio, where a presenter interviewed a local farmer.

'...a visit today from special guest, Wesley Grant, who needs no introduction to the listeners of Lantern FM. Hello Wesley, and thanks again for coming,' greeted the presenter in the kind of exaggerated voice that everybody seemed to adopt on the radio.

I bet you don't sound that happy at home. Amanda thought.

'No. Thanks for having me,' came the reply in a strong accent that made Amanda envisage a short, dumpy man in a green vest-top and wellies.

'Now, you're a bit of a veteran when it comes to running campaigns, but some say your recent stories about the Exmoor beast are rather wild and fantastical,' goaded the presenter.

'They're wild, alright... but there's nothing fantastical about stepping out on your farm and finding half your livestock's been ripped apart!' quipped Wesley.

'But surely as a farmer, road kill and attacks by foxes and other wild animals are all part and parcel of the job?' reasoned the interviewer.

'Yeah, but what we're talking about here is—'

'What we're talking about is, as one listener called it, sensationalist exaggerations of the truth that have frightened the life out of her two young children!' interrupted the presenter, sternly.

There was a momentary silence as Wesley considered his response.

'I apologise for that. I really do,' said Wesley, with genuine regret. 'But it's better to be scared and locked inside than to be out there at night. I've been on a farm all my life and what I'm seeing now, on a weekly basis, ain't no road kill. And it certainly ain't no fox!' he warned.

Amanda shook her head as she switched the radio off, letting out a tired snigger.

'Only in Devon!' she said, before pulling the curtains shut to block out the daylight.

Margaret was right. A little rest would do her good.

A pair of skeletal hands jostled through a large set of keys. They belonged to Karen Ambrose – the ghostly face that had loitered in the upstairs window upon Amanda's arrival. She took large strides – a black shadow that floated through the corridors using one hand to light the candles that hung from the walls and the other to hold a metal timepiece attached to a long, thin chain that draped deep into one of her pockets. She headed around corners, bringing dim light to each hall, before eventually entering the dining room where a large, plush table had been expertly laid out by Walter. Although the room was pre-lit, she proceeded to burn further candles on the table as her husband offered her a loving smile. She did not smile back. She merely acknowledged him – an act that left him satisfied all the same. The way Karen's eyebrows wore a constant frown and her lips remained tightly pursed, as though she were angry at something or someone, suggested she was not a woman of affection. She moved on to the kitchen, lighting candles around Margaret who cheerfully danced and sang as she prepared dinner. Karen shook her head at the woman's behaviour.

The front door represented the end of Karen's journey. She stepped outside and lit two large flames that burnt fiercely on the front porch, one either side of the door. She raised her timepiece as the second-hand whizzed around the clock face, taking the minute-hand as it passed and dropping it on the 12 to inform its owner it was now 7pm. This was indeed a finely rehearsed routine and as her watch struck seven, the entire house fell into darkness, but for the warm glow of candlelight. Karen looked out to the land around her, surveying the horizon with a territorial resistance, before stepping back inside and slamming the front door shut.

At dinner, Amanda quietly observed her new peers as they ate in silence. Amanda wondered if the atmosphere was always so stale or if it was a product of her presence. Margaret was smiling, at least, occasionally peering up from a small garment she was knitting for one of the children.

'You like it, dear?' asked Margaret in her custom motherly fashion. 'Pea and ham soup. My late husband's favourite, it was.'

'It's a shame he's not here then, isn't it?' Karen retorted, in words that dripped with venom.

The rudeness of Karen's jibe left Amanda open-mouthed, and she was shocked still further when nobody, including Margaret, batted an eyelid. Was this woman so vile that such behaviour had become normal?

'It's lovely, Margaret. Thank you,' she replied, countering Karen's bitterness with kindness.

'What do you think of the place, Amanda?' asked Walter.

'Well I haven't seen much, I'm afraid. I fell asleep in my room,' she admitted.

'Travelling does that to me, at times,' said Walter.

'Your age doesn't help!' swiped Karen.

'It was the same when I was younger, dear,' Walter pointed out, calmly, and with a dry smile upon his face.

Amanda observed the loving way Walter looked at his wife across the table, but her cold, stony eyes rarely found their way back to him. Amanda continued to study the group. She looked towards Christian, whose wedding ring was clearly visible.

'I'd never done a telephone interview before, Christian. Thanks for the experience!' said Amanda with a smile.

Christian shaped to speak.

'Oh! He don't let strangers into the house, dear,' interrupted Margaret, in the way that mums often do.

Being the person Amanda knew least about, she quickly thought of another question to throw at Christian.

'So when do I get to meet your wife?' was the first thing that sprang to mind.

She inhaled another mouthful of soup, taking a few moments to realise that the room had been filled with an awkward silence. Her eyes darted around curiously, landing on Karen, who glared at her. Walter appeared nervous and Margaret, who had laid her knitting down on the table, looked towards her son with sympathy. Christian placed his spoon on the table, taking a deep breath in order to compose himself.

'My wife…' Christian began, before stumbling. 'My wife is… no longer with us.'

Amanda looked around the room, desperately seeking guidance.

Why did nobody tell me?

'Oh! Christian! I'm so sorry. I-I didn't…'

'It's okay. Really,' he insisted, trying to perk himself up.

However, his attempt was short-lived and didn't fool anyone.

'Please excuse me,' he said, politely, before walking away from the table.

Amanda sought solace as she looked over to Margaret.

'I feel so awful,' she gasped, compassionately.

'I'm sorry, love. I should've told you,' Margaret consoled. 'Never mind. He'll be alright.'

'Well I wouldn't say that,' added Karen. 'We all know how deeply these things affect him.'

'Is there anything I can do?' asked Amanda, still reeling.

To this, Karen stood up and looked down at her. It was amazing how condescending she could be through looks alone.

'I'm tempted to say you've done enough, but as you ask, yes. Clear the table,' she instructed, before strutting out of the room with absolutely no regard for Amanda's feelings whatsoever.

It was a ruthless act that left Amanda speechless.

*

Away from the gaze of the adults, in a minimally furnished bedroom where old tattered wallpaper peeled from the walls and the naked wood on the floors was rough and dusty, hushed whispers came from a large lump under Georgina's duvet.

'K-keepsies or lendsies?' stuttered Reuben.

'Keepsies,' called Georgina.

''kay,' said Reuben in excitement as he shook his hand, through which the sound of clashing marbles could be heard.

'H-how many birds in the b-b-bush?' he asked.

'Umm… four,' she guessed.

Reuben slowly opened his hand to reveal four marbles lying in his palm.

'No… f-f-five,' he lied.

'Ah! I was close.'

'Yah!'

Reuben removed five marbles from her pile and smiled as he grouped them with his own.

Suddenly, the door burst open. The children froze and terror filled their faces. Their hearts beat loudly as footsteps rapidly neared the bed and as the cover was pulled back, Reuben looked utterly relieved to discover it was Margaret.

'What are you two doing up?' Margaret whispered. 'If Karen caught you, you'd be in trouble!'

'You won't tell on us will you?' Georgina asked, somewhat timidly.

'When've I ever done that, then?' questioned Margaret.

It was a fair point that put the children at ease.

'Now come on, Rueb,' she continued, holding out her hand. 'It's time for bed.'

He grabbed a hold of her hand and stepped onto the floor. She led him to the other side of the room, laid him down and pulled the duvet over his shoulders.

'Night-night, Georgie. Night-night, Rueb,' said Margaret, gently.

'Night Maggie,' the children responded in unison, and before they knew it, she was gone.

As the only children in the house who shared a room, they would often sneak into one another's beds. It wasn't that they were bad kids or that they had a tendency to misbehave. Far from it! They were simply afraid. It was a fear that anybody who had stayed in a large, isolated house could understand. The wind would gather and circulate around the home. At times it would howl, other times it would scream and occasionally it would whisper, waking the children from their light, anxious sleep. When this happened, it gave them the feeling they were not alone as a presence lingered in their room. Aside from this, the house would creak and screech and bang. Footsteps were a common sound throughout the house at night and the peculiar shapes and shadows that projected through the windows and onto the walls added an extra element of creepiness. On top of all this lay the fact that, just like Wesley Grant, the children knew the Exmoor beast was more than just a myth. It prowled around their home almost every night, and this was to be no exception.

CHAPTER FOUR

Mind Over Matter
Saturday 12th February, 1972

A swarm of flies buzzed relentlessly over the mangled corpse of a sheep. Its neck had been snapped and large chunks of its wool and flesh had been torn away, leaving the perfect gateway for the flies to explore the animal's insides and consider the wounds as a nesting place for their eggs.

Just a few miles away from where the poor animal lay, Amanda stirred, roused by a gentle knock at her bedroom door.

'Amanda! It's time to wake up, love,' sung Margaret with a soft grin as she poked her head round the door. 'You jump in the shower and I'll make you some breakfast.'

'Okay,' croaked Amanda, who looked at the clock to see an alien formation of numbers staring back at her – 05:58.

She buried her head under the pillows as she momentarily cussed her decision to undertake the story. The regret soon subsided though and upon taking a deep breath she forced herself out of bed.

The bathroom filled with steam as Amanda lathered her body with soap in the shower. She tilted her head back and allowed the hot water to beat off her face. The house itself was quite chilly so she found the heat rather invigorating. She recited her aims for the day: meet all of the children, press Christian when alone and make contact with Tony back at the office. She then turned the water off and pulled back the shower curtain. A young, rather peculiar-looking boy was staring right at her. Once more, she screamed, but the boy did not flinch. She reached for a nearby towel with which to cover her body.

Gordon Jones was ten-years-old and, as Amanda would later learn, was heavily autistic. Sensing that something wasn't quite right with the boy, Amanda fought hard to calm herself and spoke in a soft, unthreatening manner.

'You frightened me,' she admitted, with a light chuckle.

Gordon didn't respond in any way. He simply continued to watch her. Amanda forced an uncomfortable smile.

'I'm Amanda,' was all she could think to say, but as she stepped towards him, he turned and walked casually out of the room.

This is one hell of a mixed bag! She thought of the home's residents, as she wondered what other surprises lay in store for the rest of the day.

Margaret worked away at the stove, cracking eggs and nesting them among sizzling rashers of bacon and quarterly cut tomatoes. She insisted Amanda remain at the table as she did so.

'I can't wait for this bloody power strike to be over!' she sighed.

'It must be a real nuisance out here,' supported Amanda.

'It's gone on far too long. It goes off at two today so any chores needing electricity take priority,' Margaret stated, carrying a large plate of succulent food over to Amanda. 'The evenings can be quite testing with no electricity, but I usually pass the time by doing a bit of sewing and knitting.'

It had been only three days since the government had declared a state of emergency due to a miner's strike. That homes and businesses all over England were only allocated electricity for nine hours a day was something that really took some getting used to, although being that country life was so relaxed, it didn't cause as much disruption as it did in the city.

Margaret placed the freshly cooked breakfast in front of Amanda, viewing it with pride.

'This looks great!' Amanda enthused.

Margaret smiled as she took a seat opposite the young woman. She had no food herself and instead seemed intent on gauging Amanda's level of enjoyment.

'Where's everybody else?' Amanda asked.

'Getting the kids ready. It's been a warm winter so I expect they'd like to play outside. Oh...' said Margaret, pulling a spare set of keys from her pocket. 'Before I forget, these are for you. Now, the only rooms that have locks downstairs are Christian's office and Malcolm's bedroom. You don't have a key for the office, but Christian's usually in there anyway, so if you want to use the phone, just give him a knock.'

'That's the only phone in the house?' Amanda checked, to which

Margaret nodded.

That will make it difficult to report back to Tony.

'All the children's rooms have locks on them and I've numbered them to make it easier for you. I'll show you around upstairs later.'

Amanda took the keys, numbered 1-5, and studied them as Margaret walked out of the room.

'Wait! Did you say all their rooms have locks?' she asked, as though the words had only just sunk in.

Amanda was about to follow her when Christian entered dressed in hunting gear.

'Did you say something?' he questioned.

'Oh! I was just talking to your mother.'

'That's good,' he said, as he opened the fridge and glanced through its contents, pulling out a carton of orange juice. 'It means I don't have to!' he joked.

So far, his boyish, banterish nature did not match Amanda's perception of the man who had sounded so serious during their telephone interview. He even looked serious most of the time, making everything that came out of his mouth seem slightly ironic. It was a quirkiness that firmly held Amanda's attention.

'You're a hunter?'

'What gave it away?' he replied, shooting her a handsome grin as he poured himself a glass of juice and tipped it back his throat.

At that moment, Amanda noticed he wore a necklace with a large claw tied to the end of it.

'Ah… I have keen powers of observation,' she said. 'I guess the question should be, *what* do you hunt?'

'Oh! Just… predatory animals, you know,' he shrugged. 'Foxes scare the kids and crows are never good news.'

'So you shoot them?' she asked, a wrinkle of amusement appearing at the corner of her mouth.

'Don't think badly of me. It's better that I scare these animals away,' he assured her.

'And the necklace?' Amanda pressed, her eyes falling back to look at it.

Christian instinctively caressed the claw in his hand.

'Stupid novelty gift from my mother!' he replied. 'If I didn't put it on when I hunted, I'd never hear the end of it!'

'I wouldn't have had you down as a mamma's boy,' said Amanda, light-heartedly, as Christian slid the necklace back under his top and out of sight.

'Oh really? What would you have me down for?' he asked, his eyes meeting Amanda's amidst a glimmer of suggestion.

Margaret swirled into the room like a human tornado, carrying a basket full of laundry.

'Christian! Stop distracting the help, love. We're incredibly busy!' she said.

Christian smiled at Amanda in secret.

'And on that note, I'll see you later,' he said, raising his eyebrows before slinking out of the room.

Amanda followed Margaret out into the garden. On a wooden table, Gordon played chess with Georgina under Walter's supervision. Walter peered up from a newspaper in which he seemed deeply absorbed and smiled at the women as they approached. Amanda hesitated slightly when she saw a whole stack of papers on the floor beside him and felt flustered when he caught her staring at them.

'You must really like the news!' she blurted, feeling the need to justify her clear interest in the tabloids.

'I do-I do. And I'm always interested in how many ways the same story can be told.'

Try as she did, Amanda was unable to pry her eyes away from the pile, wondering if *The Times* lay within the collection. He seemed to have everything else. It dawned on her that an article she'd recently written – a scathing feature on Prime Minister, Edward Heath, and his vocal support of America's all-out bombing of North Vietnam – was still pending its print date. If it did come out during her stay, she would very much like to see it for reading her work when the content was so significant never failed to make her feel good.

She looked at the paper currently in his hands – a local tabloid named the *Great Western News*. The front cover was riddled with further column inches about the "Exmoor Beast."

Suddenly, half way down the pile, she saw it. *The Times*! She cleared her throat.

'Might I read them when you're done?' asked Amanda, thinking on her feet.

'Of course,' he replied.

She turned her attention towards the chess board where the children sat in total silence – Gordon moving his head back and forth between two particular positions.

'Would you mind helping me hang the washing up, dear?' asked Margaret, ever so politely.

'Of course!' Amanda agreed, before Margaret noticed her interest in the young boy.

'Oh, where are my manners? This is Gordon,' she said, believing the pair hadn't yet met.

'Gordon, huh? Another great name!'

Again, he didn't respond. Amanda leaned towards Margaret and whispered in her ear.

'What exactly is wrong with him?' she asked.

'There's nothing *wrong* with him, dear,' said Margaret who, for the first time, seemed a little incensed.

'I'm sorry. I didn't mean it like that,' reeled Amanda.

'It's okay,' Margaret relented. 'Gordon's heavily autistic. You met anyone with autism before?' she asked.

Amanda shook her head.

'Well… it's a peculiar thing, but once you get your head around it, you'll love him. He's a proper little chatter-box. Doesn't always make a lot of sense, mind you. Isn't that right, Gord?' she asked, suddenly speaking up.

'Yah!' he replied, instinctively.

Amanda studied the board, noticing that the children had yet to make a move. She approached the table and spoke gently.

'Hello, Gordon. I'm Amanda.'

'Naked lady. Yah! Gordon. My name's Gordon Jones. But naked lady can call me Gord.'

With Amanda's cheeks becoming pink and warm, she felt the need to explain.

'We… overlapped in the bathroom this morning,' she clarified, bringing a smile to Walter's face.

'Oh…' Margaret chuckled.

At least the fleeting embarrassment marked progress compared to the failed conversation she'd attempted with Gordon earlier that morning.

'Who's winning?' asked Amanda.

'It's a draw. Georgina's move,' answered Gordon, speaking at the rather manic pace he always seemed to adopt. 'She hasn't moved yet, so no-one's winning. It's a draw!'

Amanda had read about autism. Doctors had described it as a fascinating mental disease that lasted the duration of one's life and directly affected the sufferer's relationships with people – as well as the practicalities of the world – around them. Quite often, what an autistic brain lacked in social development, it more than made up for with strong short and long term memory traits, leading those who were diagnosed with it to become obsessed with numbers, patterns, statistics and routines.

'How long have you been playing?' Amanda delved.

'273 days,' he replied, instantly

'I'm sorry. I meant this game,' Amanda clarified.

'Yah, 273 days. Started 15th May, 1971,' he confirmed.

'You started *this* game last May?' repeated Amanda.

'Yah. 15th May, 1971: 273 days. Georgina's turn,' he said.

Amanda's focus shifted to the girl.

'Are you going to make a move today, Georgina?' she asked.

Georgina didn't reply, which led Walter to glare disapprovingly over the top of his paper.

'Georgina?' he said, slowly, menacingly.

Walter lowered his paper entirely and leant forward in his chair, making the old wood creek as he did so.

'Answer,' he said, through gritted teeth.

It was the first time Amanda had seen Walter irked and suddenly he gave off the energy of someone who could have a temper.

'I'm thinking!' Georgina snapped.

In a slow, calculated manner, Walter leant back in his chair with his eyes still locked on her. His nose twitched before he returned to his paper.

'H-m,' he grunted, and that was that.

Margaret nodded further down the garden where a washing line hung across the lawn and together, the women walked away.

'Sorry, dear. She has good days and bad, that one,' confirmed Margaret. 'Yesterday was a particularly good day.'

'They play chess?'

'Well "play" is a bit of a loose term for it! You know, it's the strangest thing. The chess board lay under the stairs and hadn't been touched for years. One day, out of the blue, they both asked to play it in the garden and they've insisted on doing it ever since. I don't know where they got the idea from. Can't think they'd even know how to play. I don't even know! They seem to enjoy it, though. Whatever you do, you mustn't touch the pieces. I learnt that the hard way!' she said, rolling her eyes.

As Margaret picked up speed, Amanda glanced back towards the children.

Interesting!

Amanda couldn't quite put her finger on what it was yet, but something was most definitely amiss. She looked forward to the end of the day, by which time she would have visited each room of the house and stared into the eyes of every child. Once this was done, she would be able to do what she did best – get to the bottom of the story, and generate some theories on what it was that made the residents act so utterly peculiar.

CHAPTER FIVE

The Secret Garden

Saturday 12th February, 1972

Further along the garden was the clothes line, stretched between two poles that lay a considerable distance apart. As the women got closer, Amanda could hear the slow and constant squeak of an old rusty swing-set coming from a secluded garden. Sat on the swing was a tall, gaunt boy named Malcolm Keane.

'What's he doing out here alone?' complained Margaret as she dropped the basket and headed towards him.

Amanda followed.

Even with both women there, Malcolm didn't stir. Instead, he gazed motionlessly into space as he swung somewhat hypnotically, not even sparing the energy to blink. Beside him was an old wheelchair that Amanda guessed was used for his transportation.

'Amanda, this is Malcolm. What you see is what you get. In all the time he's been here, he's never shown much sign of progression. If anything, he's gotten worse. It's as if he simply doesn't even know he's alive,' she said.

'What do you mean?'

'Well, he's been here for six years and he hasn't acknowledged anything around him for four of them. The doctors think he may have been the victim of severe abuse as a child and it made him create his own world that he doesn't wanna come out of,' said Margaret.

Amanda couldn't help but feel saddened.

'What happened to his parents?' she asked.

'What happened to all of their parents?' Margaret shrugged. 'We just don't know. All our residents were either neglected or abandoned because their conditions were deemed too demanding.'

'Do they ever get visitors?' Amanda probed.

'No. The cold hard fact is nobody cares about them. They were too much to care for and nobody's interested in fostering a child that requires so much attention. That's where we come in,' said Margaret, revealing elements of both pride and resolve. 'We're their family now.'

As Amanda looked back at Malcom, she was caught by an unexpected wave of emotion.

How badly must someone have been abused to completely give up? She pondered. A storm of emotions built in her heart and tears began to form in her eyes.

'Any parent who stands by and just...'

Amanda fell into an outraged silence.

'I know, dear,' whispered Margaret, ever so gently, as she patted her on the back. 'I know.'

Emotionally, it appeared that Margaret and Amanda were kindred spirits and for both women, just knowing that somebody shared their own grief proved some form of consolation. They both kept an eye on Malcolm as they clipped the washing to the line. The sky was an odd combination of purple and grey, yet it was warm. Indeed, Exmoor seemed to make up its own rules when it came to the climate. Now that Amanda was stood there, she noticed an outhouse partially hidden behind a row of hedges at the foot of the hill.

'Does that belong to the home?' she asked.

'Sure does,' Margaret confirmed.

'What's in there?' Amanda snooped.

'Well, most of the building's used for storage, but it's also where our groundskeeper lives.'

'Groundskeeper? I haven't seen him,' said Amanda.

'Oh, he's a very private man. Goes about his business quietly,' Margaret informed her.

'What's his name?'

'Arthur. You'll see him around from time to time, I'm sure. Try not to disturb him though, eh? He doesn't much like conversation.'

Amanda nodded and proceeded to hang up the washing. Indeed, it was Margaret that seemed to linger on the topic.

'He's a lovely man. Lonely, but lovely,' she added.

The morning had enhanced Amanda's knowledge of the home considerably, but not until Margaret led her beyond the car park and through a flowery archway towards a very subtle outdoor enclosure did she experience genuine surprise. The land was so beautifully preserved that the last thing she expected to see was the home's very own graveyard, where scores of headstones stood in pristine condition.

'What is this?' gasped Amanda, clearly shaken.

'Where'd you think they went once they'd passed on, dear?' asked Margaret, as though it was the most logical conclusion in the world.

'In a graveyard!' replied Amanda, passionately.

'This is a graveyard,' stated Margaret.

'Who sanctioned this?' Amanda continued, sounding far more aggravated than she had intended.

'What does that matter, lovely?' asked Margaret.

'It's… not right!'

'What? Burying them with the only people who ever really cared about them? I can't think of anything more fitting,' she countered, looking over the headstones as though reliving fond memories of the deceased.

Amanda took a moment to absorb the information. Something about the situation didn't sit well with her at all, but then, as she saw Margaret's reaction – the way the yard seemed to bring her peace – she wondered if she should be more liberal. She took a deep breath and attempted to remain neutral, but she needed to know more.

'How did they die?' she eventually asked, in a more relaxed manner.

'Well, when we first established the home we housed terminally ill children, but it just got too much. Losing people you love on what was nearly a monthly basis was… very tough,' she sighed.

'I've never heard of a home that does this,' interjected Amanda, unable to conceal her shock.

'Well, they should,' said Margaret, adamantly. 'We're the only people to care for these children in life, so it's only right we do the same in death. I'm sorry if you find it strange, my love.'

Margaret was a clear advocate of keeping the bodies within the grounds and Amanda could tell she had offended Margaret by her reaction. Now that she had explained things from her point-of-view, though, Amanda could understand her opinion. The question of where the bodies should have been laid to rest, if not there, wasn't an easy one to answer. Amanda wondered what it was about Margaret that made even the most bizarre of situations understandable. She looked to the ground and shifted on her feet, feeling bad for upsetting a woman who was so loving and caring.

'It just took me by surprise, that's all,' Amanda admitted, offering some form of apology.

Margaret being Margaret immediately found a way to forgive her.

'I guess that's understandable, love… but Christian used to be in the funeral business, see?'

This was news to Amanda.

'Really?' she remarked, flippantly, but deeply interested.

'Yeah. My husband was an undertaker and, years ago, he began his own funeral business. It was successful, too! When Christian left school, he wanted nothing more than to work with his dad. It wasn't long before they were partners and the business grew like wild fire. He has the gift of the gab, does Christian. People just seem to warm to him. They trust him. They worked together for years and made a lot of money. A *lot* of money!'

'What was your husband's name?' asked Amanda, curiously.

Stanley Prince was his name. It said so on his headstone, and if his doting wife was happy to bury her husband in the yard then maybe it wasn't such a twisted idea after all.

STANLEY PRINCE
A LOYAL HUSBAND AND LOVING FATHER
FOREVER IN OUR HEARTS
1902–1967

'He died of a heart attack, bless him,' revealed Margaret. Amanda rubbed her back with affection.

'Where did you meet?' asked Amanda, hoping to provoke a fond memory.

'I was working as a carer in Kent, looking after kids who'd been affected by violence in a place called Saint Matthews.'

Hearing the name aloud sent a shudder down Amanda's spine. Saint Matthews is where she had been sent immediately after her mother overdosed on pills, a suspected suicide that had left her all alone. It was the beginning of several lonely years for Amanda, during which the one person she remembered fondly was stood before her, engrossed in telling her story.

'I went into town one day for lunch and this man rode his pushbike right into a lamppost. I, of course, rushed over to help. Turns out he hit the lamppost because he was looking at me!' she chuckled.

Amanda smiled along.

'Oh! He was a fool!' continued Margaret. 'But he was my fool. And the bond he had with Christian was unbreakable.'

After another short moment of gazing at her husband's grave, Margaret dusted herself down and took a deep breath.

'Anyway… I'd better show you the rest of the house.'

Amanda observed Margaret closely as she explained certain homely routines. Her sadness soon subsided and she seemed to have an extra spring in her step. Thinking about it, Margaret must have been over the moon to have somebody to talk to given the rest of the characters that ordinarily surrounded her. Amanda knew their growing friendship was a real asset but didn't feel good about exploiting such an affectionate source for the sake of a story. If she had a choice, she would find the information through other means.

They took Malcolm to his bedroom, where Amanda used her key for door number 1. It was the only child's room on the ground floor and situated directly opposite Christian's bedroom. Margaret then led Amanda back up the stairs to the first floor where she learnt that room 2 was occupied by Reuben and Georgina, who were the only children that shared, room 3 belonged to Gordon and room 4 belonged to David, who she had yet to meet. There was nothing really special about the rooms except for the fact the quality of the décor seemed to decrease the further up the house they travelled. Amanda found this fascinating as she had long harboured an interest in the Victorian era, where this would be common practice among wealthy families. Back then, the rich would stay in well-decorated rooms towards the ground floor of the house and the servants would often be confined to small, makeshift rooms further up and towards the attic. Amanda wondered if the reason the children's rooms were so poorly decorated was a clue towards their destructive nature – a theory supported by Margaret as she turned and faced Amanda at the end of the hall.

'And this is number 5,' Margaret said, stopping outside the door and looking Amanda directly in the eyes. 'This is Ellie's room. Now don't be scared and try not to get too upset by her behaviour,' she added, rather ominously.

'Why? What's wrong with—'

Margaret shot Amanda a look that reminded her to rephrase the question.

'Sorry! I mean… what's her condition?' asked Amanda.

'She's deeply depressed. Suicidal. And she can be *very* aggressive,' Margaret informed her.

'Suicidal? How old is she?'

'Fourteen,' Margaret replied. 'Now, because she don't know you, she may attack you, but it's only because she's scared. If she does, don't panic! We'll just have to restrain her for a few seconds and she'll calm down. Alright?'

It wasn't alright at all, but Amanda fought hard not to look as overwhelmed as she felt, watching anxiously as Margaret took the lead and inserted a key into the lock.

Clunk!

Cautiously, they both entered the room, which was almost completely bare except for a bed and a large wooden wardrobe.

'Ellie?' called Margaret, softly.

She flicked the light switch but the specialised plastic light that clung to the centre of the ceiling sparked and faded.

A very small window was positioned high up on the far wall, providing the only source of brightness and ventilation. At first glance, it was as though squatters had broken in and taken residence in an old empty building. Visibility was low and Amanda had to squint, forcing her eyes to adjust. When she could see more clearly, she noticed that the walls were padded with cushions. She couldn't resist pressing her hand against the material, a spongy padding that was about three inches thick at the centre of each panel.

'Ellie?' Margaret repeated, patiently, as she moved around the room in search of the youngster.

There was still no answer.

'Where are you, my lovely?' she continued, in a gentle tone that insinuated they were playing a game. 'Under the bed?'

Amanda watched closely as Margaret approached the mattress and shaped to crouch under it.

'There's someone I want you to meet,' she said, struggling to lower herself to her knees before exploring the darkness under the bed for what seemed like an eternity.

There was a sudden *Thump!* as Ellie Sullivan burst out of the wardrobe and ran at Amanda, screaming at the top of her lungs as she rapidly approached her. When their bodies came together, the impact was fierce and Ellie lashed out in a ferocious rage.

'Ellie! Stop it!' yelled Margaret, as she fought her way back to her feet and grabbed a hold of the young girl's flailing arms.

It didn't stop her. Instead, Ellie started to kick out at Amanda, who stood dumbstruck as she was hit by a barrage of blows.

'Grab her feet!' instructed Margaret.

It took a moment for the words to register, but eventually Amanda managed to get a good grip of the girl and together, she and Margaret struggled towards the bed. Ellie's pulsating body made the task incredibly difficult. Eventually they pinned her down but her level of fight increased as she squirmed, spat and screamed hysterically at the women. The struggle was such that Amanda wondered if they could be heard in the room beneath.

Thump!

Bang!

Thrwack!

Ellie hissed viciously, like a powerful snake that turned every which way in an attempt to break free. The look in her eyes was frightening and Amanda wondered what she would be capable of should she manage to elude their grip.

'Calm down, my lovely. Calm down. She's not gonna hurt you,' insisted Margaret.

Whether the words acted as some kind of reassurance, or whether the girl had simply fought herself to exhaustion, Ellie's struggle weakened to a series of sporadic jolts.

'She works for us now. She's gonna live with us,' Margaret

informed Ellie, gently brushing her hand over the girl's sweat-drenched brow.

Slowly but surely, Ellie calmed. Amanda took a moment to catch her breath and noticed that the youngster's arms were covered in cuts and scratches. Some of the markings were permanent scars caused from deep and nasty wounds. It was certainly a sight worthy of Amanda's concern.

When Margaret was satisfied it was safe enough to leave her, she led Amanda back out into the hallway and routinely locked the door. Amanda was quiet. The shock of being attacked had shaken her more than she would have guessed. The girl was so young! That's what got to her most.

How can someone so young be so unhappy?

Sensing Amanda's hazy state of mind, Margaret didn't push for conversation. Instead, she offered a consoling smile, as if to say everything would be okay, before heading back towards the staircase. Suddenly, Amanda snapped out of her daze, looking over her shoulder towards the hallway that continued around the corner from Ellie's room, fading into darkness as though it had been forgotten.

'What's around here?' she asked, stepping towards a better vantage point before Margaret could reply.

Amanda saw that it led to a dark and narrow staircase, at the top of which stood a small but heavy door.

'Oh! We don't need to worry about that,' insisted Margaret, continuing to inch towards the stairs.

Something, however, kept Amanda's attention on the door. She didn't know why, but she had an inexplicable urge to know what was inside. Every other part of the house had either been shown to Amanda, or at very least had its contents and its purpose explained, but not the attic. Amanda looked at her keys: five keys for the five bedrooms that slept six children. There was no key for this small, intriguing door that had a large and robust lock attached to the outside, as though it were guarding some great hidden secret. Wishing to keep her insatiable curiosity under wraps, Amanda placed her keys in her pocket and followed Margaret, slinking down the stairs behind her, but she was determined to come back and explore the secret room at the first possible chance she got.

*External grounds, the Prince Care Home - 1972

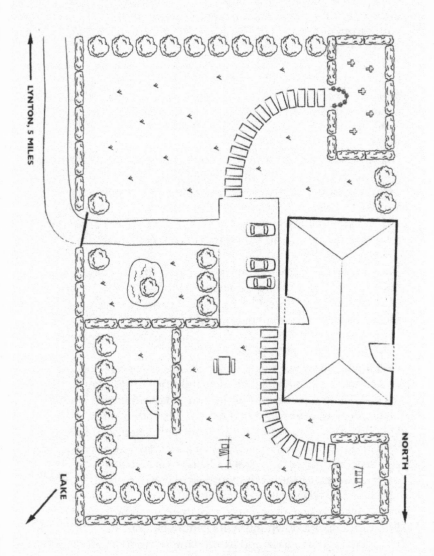

*Internal blueprint, the Prince Care Home - 1972

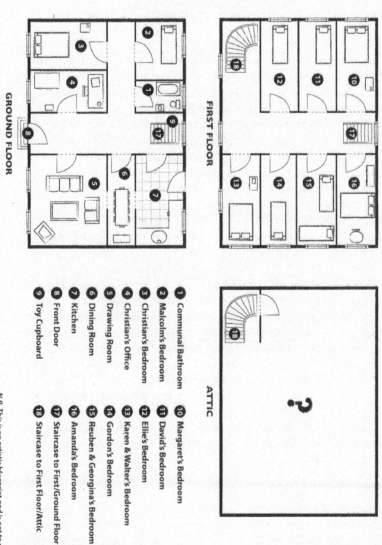

GROUND FLOOR

FIRST FLOOR

ATTIC

1. Communal Bathroom
2. Malcolm's Bedroom
3. Christian's Bedroom
4. Christian's Office
5. Drawing Room
6. Dining Room
7. Kitchen
8. Front Door
9. Toy Cupboard
10. Margaret's Bedroom
11. David's Bedroom
12. Ellie's Bedroom
13. Karen & Walter's Bedroom
14. Gordon's Bedroom
15. Reuben & Georgina's Bedroom
16. Amanda's Bedroom
17. Staircase to First/Ground Floor
18. Staircase to First Floor/Attic

N.B. This is an artistic blueprint and is not to scale.

CHAPTER SIX

Lights Out
Saturday 12th February, 1972

In front of the soft glow of the open fire, Gordon, Reuben and Georgina lay fast asleep on the large, comfy sofa. Malcolm sat before a nearby window and simply stared out into space. Margaret looked to Walter and indicated he was to take Malcolm to bed. She then looked at Amanda and nodded towards Gordon. Margaret herself tended to Reuben, lifting his light frame over her shoulder before nudging Georgina, who stirred with a light groan. Together, they manoeuvred around the room in well-synchronised silence.

Gordon was of a very slight build and therefore easy enough to carry. Amanda opened his bedroom door and entered the room, into which the soft blue moonlight shone. The sky outside was dark and stormy and the wind was picking up. Amanda placed Gordon delicately into bed, pulled his blanket over him and swept his hair gently across his forehead. She watched him for a moment and became lost in quiet emotion. Never had she been very maternal, yet there she was, finding genuine comfort in the child's well-being and swooning at the sight of his peaceful sleep. Before she had a chance to analyse where her inner warmth had stemmed from, Gordon stirred.

'Lights out. Eight o'clock,' he instructed.

She couldn't help but chuckle at the boy's manner. He was so deeply humorous and sweet.

'It's alright. It's not eight just yet, Gord,' she informed him.

'Oh!' he said, unsure of what to make of the information.

'You look tired,' she said, softly.

'Yah. Tired. I'm definitely a little tired. Lights out, eight o'clock.'

She smiled before shaping to leave.

'Where's Elijah?' asked Gordon.

Amanda looked back at him, wondering if he was caught in a dream, but he seemed quite awake and was looking expectantly towards the window.

'Who's Elijah?'

'The dog. He's the dog.'

'You have a dog?' Amanda questioned.

'Yah!'

'How come I haven't seen him, Gord?'

'He comes to my window every night. He comes to help me sleep,' the boy claimed.

Amanda instinctively walked over to the window and absorbed the view. His room was only two along from hers, so offered a similar perspective of the land, but this time she observed in greater detail. A drainpipe ran down the house nearby and a strip of wooden slatted fencing held some shrubbery in place against the wall. Although it would be dangerous, a person might be able to climb to Gordon's window using these for assistance, but a dog? Impossible!

'The dog comes to your window?'

'Yah! I can't sleep without him,' he told her.

'We're upstairs, Gord,' said Amanda, curious as to whether this would affect his certainty.

'Yah!' he said, without a second thought.

Amanda took a moment to choose her words.

'So… what does it look like? Your dog?' she coaxed.

'Like this,' replied Walter, making Amanda's heart skip a beat as he ghosted into the room carrying a small teddy bear.

'Vivid imagination, this one!' he continued as he handed the cuddly toy to Gordon.

'Yah. The dog comes to my room. I can't sleep without him,' he muttered, taking the bear before rolling onto his side.

Some leads were promising. Most were not. Amanda placed the notion of Gordon having a dog firmly in the latter category, although the toy he held was a bear, not a dog, and she'd be suprised if somebody as particular as him didn't know the difference.

'Goodnight Gord,' she said with affection, before leaving the room with Walter.

*

49

In the company of a large glass of milk and a burning lantern, Amanda sat manically scribbling notes into her notepad.

I am yet to witness any questionable means of discipline, but several unorthodox procedures are in place, was one statement.

I was deeply concerned by the marks on Ellie's arms, yet her frighteningly aggressive nature gives me no reason to suspect they weren't self-inflicted, was another.

Ever since she had discovered the graveyard, her opinion as to whether or not its inclusion within the grounds was ethical had changed more often than the direction of the wind.

The graveyard poses many questions. I need to explore Christian's background as an undertaker, was the final summary of her conflict, but with the issue firmly lodged in her mind, she walked towards her window and looked outside. She could see the swing, the washing line and a section of the outhouse down the bottom of the garden but the flowery archway she desired was situated on the other side of the house. Still, the view appeared creepy enough at night, especially with the wind giving artificial movement to everything in sight. Goosebumps spread over her skin as she thought about the bodies that lay under the yard. It was terrifying but engaging at the same time – enough to lead her outside, at least.

The grass crunched beneath Amanda's feet as she made her way through the flowery archway and towards the headstones. She held a lantern close in one hand and grasped her Dictaphone tightly in the other. The rusty squeaking of the swing carried through the yard, sending an eerie chill down her spine.

Once in the graveyard, she studied the headstone directly next to Stanley's.

LYDIA PRINCE
TO A WONDERFUL WIFE AND DAUGHTER
MAY YOU BE AT PEACE WITH THE ANGELS
1934–1960

Amanda pulled the Dictaphone to her lips.

'I questioned Margaret about Christian's wife, but said she didn't feel comfortable talking about it. *Didn't feel comfortable*?

What an odd expression,' she reflected.

She ran her hand over the headstone.

'The headstones are old, yet look as good as new. They're detailed in their design and have—'

Amanda stopped immediately as she heard the front door to the house shut. She edged back towards the archway where she could watch in secret as Christian – again dressed in his hunting gear – rummaged around in the boot of his jeep before closing the door with care. He climbed into the driver's seat and, somewhat peculiarly, released the handbrake so the vehicle rolled quietly down the hill. Not until he was near the gate at the bottom did he start the engine and turn on the headlights, which pierced through the dark fields ahead of his jeep. It was 1:20am.

'I know you're not hunting for crows now!' said Amanda, under her breath.

As Amanda stepped back towards the house she ducked into the shadows when she noticed Karen peering out of her bedroom window, watching Christian's jeep closely as it disappeared into the distance. Seeming agitated, Karen yanked the curtains shut.

What are you up to? Amanda pondered.

Amanda's belief that something unsavoury was happening increased with every passing minute. Suddenly, her mind was ablaze with questions and conspiracy theories. She knew she should rest and start afresh in the morning, but she was running out of time, for it was already the early hours of Sunday morning – the day she'd promised Tony she would make her excuses and leave. She already knew this would not be possible. Not until she'd discovered what the homeowners were up to.

With great caution, she walked through the main hallway on the ground floor of the home, her lantern guiding her through the darkness. She feared that Karen would exit her room and catch her wandering around, but Amanda was in a super vigilant state and couldn't detect any movement or sound. Therefore, she crept up the staircase to the first floor, controlling her breathing and making painstaking efforts not to allow the boards to creak beneath her feet. She reached the top of the stairs and stopped for a moment. If anybody caught her there, she would have plausible deniability as she was right outside her bedroom and could claim she needed to visit the lavatory. However, every step she took further down the hallway would make her proximity more difficult to explain, and the staircase that she wanted to explore was right opposite Walter and Karen's bedroom. Should they come out and see her there, Amanda would not be able to deny the fact she was snooping. She took one small step. Then another. She gulped as her eyes darted between Karen's bedroom door and the impossible darkness that seeped from around the corner. Not even a window, tinted through apparent neglect, effected the darkness that stalked the attic door. It was as though it belonged to another world.

Amanda found it funny how people could be so afraid of the dark, as though somewhere within it was the chance of being confronted by their greatest nightmares. Her breaths became heavy as she crept along, feeling anxious that her every move could be heard. She had made it half way down the hallway and was listening intently for any movement coming from Karen's room, but it remained silent. This was her chance. She was ready. She glanced around the hallway one last time to make sure she was alone, but she wasn't alone, for right at the end of the hallway, peering through the window and staring directly at her was a vicious snarling animalistic being, and it was angry.

Amanda's lantern dropped to the floor and smashed on the ground as, for the third time during her short stay, she screamed.

In the midst of the darkness, precisely as she feared, she had met something from a nightmare.

CHAPTER SEVEN

Left Behind

Thursday 10th – Sunday 13th February, 1972

Telling Amanda he loved her had not gone according to plan.

Tony sank the remnants of a second bottle of red wine, deciding that was probably enough for the evening. He rinsed out his glass in his new state-of-the-art kitchen. Bright green and orange tiles surrounded him – purposefully chosen colours selected in the belief their vibrancy would help keep him in good spirits.

On that particular day, it wasn't working.

He stumbled around his dimly lit house, casting his eye over all the things that lay around him. For the previous two years he'd allocated a quarter of his salary to improving the home. He'd bought the perfect leather chair to help him work at the desk in his study, a bespoke modern bookshelf was filled with his favourite works of fiction, the entire easterly wall of his house was made up of glass, a well-researched collection of foreign plants added something exotic to every room and inspirational pieces of modern art were strategically placed around the home to keep him mentally stimulated at all times. He'd even recently painted a rather striking two-tone stripe that lay horizontally across the middle of every supporting wall in the house. One stripe was chocolate brown and the other bright orange. Bright orange – the colour of the Dutch football kit – was his favourite colour. You could tell this immediately by visiting his home and stepping into his garage where the most recent of his extravagant purchases – a Volkswagen Beetle – sat safely polished, waiting keenly to be used.

Tony had worked hard to support his frivolous lifestyle. He hadn't realised it until now, but the thrill of buying such new-fangled things and subsequently becoming the centre of attention had become something of an addiction for him. Upon wondering why, he concluded that the feeling of importance it gave him successfully masked the fact he lived something of a lonely life.

He was handsome and endlessly charming, able to hold the attention of any room – be it at work or in a more playful setting. In fact, so charming was he that he was never perceived as a show-off. People just gravitated towards him and quickly warmed to his charismatic nature. They trusted his endearing smile. He was interesting and, when he wasn't talking, he was listening intently. Not everybody could do both, so people loved him for it.

In the cold light of day, though, what did he really have?

The more he thought about it, the more he realised nothing had enriched his life in the same way Amanda did. Everything he owned was worthless without her. Even the great pride he took in becoming the Senior Editor at *The Times*, one of the biggest newspapers in the world, was only thought of with such fond nostalgia because it was the job that had brought him and Amanda together.

'I love you more than anything in the world,' he had said. 'And I'm ready to start a family.'

As he relived the speech he'd delivered so brazenly – speaking as though Amanda should drop to her knees in gratitude and look up to him in awe – he could only cringe. How smug and arrogant he must have appeared to her, the one woman whose strength and integrity he truly admired. She was disappointed in him. He could see it in her eyes, and as she thought of a way to escape his overbearing grip on her, he became immediately regretful of the way he had approached the proposal. His only saving grace was that, until that moment, he had never acted in such a presumptuous way.

The thing that made Tony such a good editor was that he could always find truth, be it through a person's dialogue or through the way they acted. Like a seasoned detective, he could read a person's body language, finding information in the silences as well as through their words. He had an almost scientific understanding of the things people did when telling a lie and when Amanda had cut their evening short by claiming she was tired, he knew it was because she simply needed to be away from him.

Among his many sexual conquests, he had notched quite a few interns down the years as he made his way up the journalistic ladder, but he had always maintained a strict rule against sleeping with permanent colleagues. It was never a good idea to mix business with pleasure. He was an intelligent man and knew relationships were hard enough even when one only saw their partner after work during the least stressful hours of their day, so courting somebody within the office never seemed a smart thing to do.

Amanda, though, was the kind of character that tended to alter opinions. Often, men within the editor's office would scoff at the idea of female journalists and reporters. "The industry's too competitive!" misogynistic writers would say. "They wouldn't be able to keep up," claimed others. "Women are too bitchy," "...over-emotional" and "...lazy," made up a list of further common assumptions. Although Tony was more progressive than most, he had seen very little evidence during his career to counter such sexist claims. Ordinarily, during Tony's time at the paper, women only applied for secretarial roles and so when Amanda put herself forward for a job as junior content writer, he was only too happy to meet her. Being that he was a fair man who judged people on individual merit, he found the idea of female writers a refreshing one and believed it would help bring some much needed balance to his news team.

From the moment Tony entered the reception area to greet Amanda for her interview he was absolutely taken by her beauty. When she spoke, he used his powers of observation to discover the things most others would fail to detect. She was intelligent, that was undeniable. It couldn't be missed as it was the persona she wanted people to see, but Tony sensed it was mainly a mask behind which she could hide. Deep down, she was vulnerable, something she buried through assertion, and the authority with which she spoke only served to disguise her need for guidance. She was hurting; quite why wasn't so clear, but this hurt was the reason she had become so driven. Tony read her as clear as day and didn't hesitate in giving her the job. He knew he had feelings for her ever since that first encounter, so his intention was to keep her at a distance in the workplace. He treated Amanda with respect and admired her as a professional, and such was the quality of her work that she gave him no choice but to promote her, meaning they began working together more closely. As time went by, it became clear his feelings were reciprocated. It was such a thing of beauty to fall in love with someone so similar, and their mutual resistance inevitably gave way.

The first kiss they shared – late at night when, as usual, they were the only people left in the office – moved the earth beneath their feet. These two tortured souls who genuinely believed they were alone in the world had found their counter point and suddenly, together, they contemplated the possibility of sharing their lives with another.

These were the memories that deepened his unrest.

I'll sleep on it. He thought. *I can turn things around in the morning when she calls from Devon.*

The morning soon came and Tony sat anxiously by the phone in his office. The red wine had given him a throbbing headache, his eyes were bloodshot and his skin was pale. He was unable to even contemplate breakfast and focusing on work was impossible as his attentions continued to drift back to the silent handset that lay on his desk. When it eventually rang, he couldn't answer quickly enough.

'Hey!' he said, softly, holding back the reservoir of words that were fighting to pass through his lips. 'How was the journey?' was the combination he eventually chose.

'It was okay,' Amanda replied, sounding dejected.

Tony's heart skipped a beat. He was worried. Was it a bad journey or was her tone more a reflection on how she felt towards him?

'The train pulled in early if you can believe… shit!' she cussed.

She was clearly irritable. Tony knew this only happened when she was experiencing particularly bad period pains or if she was incredibly pissed off with someone, which wasn't very often.

'What's wrong?' he asked, secretly terrified of what she might say.

The phone crackled as he spoke.

'What?' barked Amanda, sounding even more agitated.

'What's wrong?' he repeated.

She fell silent. Tony closed his eyes and lowered his head, feeling certain the next words out of her mouth would be along the lines of *'Listen, I've been thinking, and maybe we should give each other a little space.'*

'Sorry. The line's pretty bad,' she eventually replied. 'Nothing's wrong. I'm fine,' she insisted, but Tony knew her better than anyone, and he knew this was a lie.

He fell silent. He thought hard but didn't know what else to say. It was the only time he could recall there being an awkward silence between them. He feared it represented the end of their relationship.

'I wish I could believe it,' said Tony.

'Fine! Everything. Everything's wrong!' she snapped. 'Tony, I…'

'Hey! It's okay. We'll be okay,' he insisted.

Now, it was his turn to lie. The truth was, he didn't know they would be okay at all, but he did know that as long as there was a fighting chance, he would never give up on what they had. This *was* the woman he wanted to marry. She *was* the one he wanted to start a family with. He would never force the issue again but that didn't change the fact it was true and he knew that as long as they were together, he would be happy. He leaned forward and used all of his might to sound optimistic and relaxed as he spoke.

'You'll be back in three days,' Tony reminded her. 'We can talk then. Okay?'

'I guess,' she huffed.

He convinced himself he shouldn't read too much into her deflated voice as she may very well have felt the same as him. Therefore, he picked it up another level.

'And that's *three* days. You'll be back here on Sunday as agreed. Okay?' instructed Tony.

'Yeah,' she accepted, softly.

'Because I know what you're like when you get your teeth into something and if you try to go back on your word, I'll come down there and pull you out myself!' he continued.

'Yes, boss! Message received,' she replied, playfully.

He could picture her smile.

The relief was overwhelming.

Maybe all was not yet lost.

'I do love you,' he said.

'You too,' she replied, driving Tony to secret tears.

That was Friday, and the way the conversation ended meant he did manage to get his work done, after all. However, the rest of Friday past, as did Saturday, without the hint of a whisper. Then, on Sunday, at the same time, on the same desk, Tony sat staring at his phone, reliving the emotions all over again. The morning had been tense and, perhaps wrongfully, he skipped his lunch. The afternoon crept by at an abnormally slow pace and every time he checked his watch it felt as though time had stood still, but eventually, in the early stage of the evening, the call he had been waiting for finally came through.

CHAPTER EIGHT

Seldom Late

Sunday 13th February, 1972

It was 05:50 and Margaret would be in to wake Amanda at any moment, but there was no need. She'd barely slept a wink all night. She'd apologised to Margaret, Walter and Karen, who all appeared with haste upon hearing her screams on the first floor landing. The best excuse she could muster was that she thought she'd heard one of the children stirring after visiting the kitchen to get some water, at which point she completely overreacted to a nearby shadow. If the words had come from Amanda Connors, she would have felt embarrassed, but Amanda Green was quite comfortable disclosing such details. The explanation seemed to satisfy them. All except Karen, at least, who Amanda always felt was watching her with suspicion.

The incident scuppered Amanda's desire to return to the attic doorway as being caught there twice in one night would have been far too revealing. In truth, though, there were two matters that had become more pressing. The first was the identity of the ghastly creature that watched Amanda through the window. She was short-sighted and the hallway was dark, but she knew she saw *something*. Being that she was so tired, she felt a little paranoid and chose not to mention the sighting to the other residents. In any case, something told her they were all too aware of what lay outside on the moors. Indeed, if they did know about such a grisly beast occupying the land, Christian's late-night hunting ventures suddenly made a lot more sense.

The second pressing matter was that ever since Amanda first bled at the age of thirteen, her menstrual cycle ran like clockwork – always on a Saturday, every four weeks. She had spent much of her adolescence marvelling at how her body operated so reliably and efficiently and not once had her cycle changed, until that very day.

She lay in bed and thought of what it would mean to be

pregnant. How odd the timing would be given that Tony had just been so forward in telling her of his desire to start a family. For hours, Amanda had been running through her list of reasons as to why the news would be a catastrophe, but after viewing each of her concerns objectively, she found there were surprisingly few things that caused her to worry.

She lifted the covers and peered down to her stomach. It didn't look particularly different. She didn't really *feel* any different, although she remembered how peculiar she had felt when watching Gordon sleep and wondered if it was Mother Nature's way of preparing her for things to come.

'I love you more than anything in the world. And I'm ready to start a family.' That's what Tony had told her the night before she left London. He had even gone to the trouble of booking the nicest table at her favourite restaurant – a quaint little family-run eatery down St. Martin's Lane in Soho, which served the finest Italian food she had ever encountered. Tony's words had surprised her. She had a naive assumption that as Tony was so similar to her he would be happy to keep plodding along without the need for such a major commitment. As she looked back, she was ashamed to admit that his outpour of emotions had made her feel suffocated. Ever since that night, she had been haunted by her reaction. He said such lovely things and she responded by running away.

How could she do that to the man she so loved?

She recalled Margaret's description of meeting her husband. She remembered the fondness in her face when she said *'He was a fool! But he was my fool.'* Tony would have undoubtedly felt foolish as he mumbled descriptions of his feelings - such foreign words to his tongue – in the restaurant. At the time, the words seemed so threatening, but as Amanda looked back they were utterly endearing.

I've found my fool! She thought, and as she placed her hands on her belly, inexplicable warmth radiated from inside her and consumed her entire body. The insatiable quest to ensure children were kept safe and that the sanctity of family was preserved lay at her very fingertips, and against all odds, she was to be the head of that family.

With a gentle wrap at the door, Margaret poked her head inside.

'Amanda. Time to wake up, my love,' she sang once more.

'I'm awake,' replied Amanda, joyfully, smiling in mellow bliss.

*

Within Christian's office, the telephone rang. It was loud and its shrill could be heard out in the hall, prompting Karen to march towards the door and unlock it with haste, her bony hand picking up the receiver.

'Yes?' she said, in an unfriendly, unapologetic voice.

It was hardly a surprise when nobody answered. The line, however, remained live, as though somebody were on the other end, listening with intent.

'Hello? Hello?' Karen hissed, deeply exasperated, before slamming the phone down.

Karen took a moment to collect her thoughts before leaving the room with purpose, locking the door behind her, as she always did. She stormed outside and headed directly towards Christian, who pulled a cloth from a large bucket of soapy water and slapped it against his filthy jeep.

'It happened again,' spat Karen, expressing her concern.

'What did?' he asked, casually.

'The phone calls,' she said, as though he should have known what she was talking about.

'I told you, you're reading too much into it,' insisted Christian as he washed the grime away with small circular movements, taking great care of his vehicle.

*

Across the lawn, Amanda sat reading the morning papers with Walter, having plucked *The Times* from his grasp. Reading her colleagues' work somehow made her feel close to Tony as she fondly envisaged what squabbles would have taken place in the office since her departure.

After a quick scan of the headlines, she returned it to Walter.

Her attention then drifted to the local papers, where more articles had been published regarding the Exmoor beast.

I wonder... She thought, connecting the stories to the inexplicable sighting she had the previous evening, but the fantasy of having encountered the legendary being was distracted by the intensity with which Karen spoke to Christian in the car park. They were just about within earshot but Amanda had to read their body language for most of the exchange.

'I'm telling you, it's her!' she believed Karen said, before Christian shrugged and Karen said something about *'...a feeling,'* to which Christian seemed to quip *'I didn't think you had any feelings.'*

At that, Karen spun on her heels and stropped back into the house.

'It was a joke!' Christian added, audibly and somewhat cheekily, but it was too late. She was gone.

His indifference to Karen's mood swings was something Amanda found thoroughly amusing, but she didn't give herself long to enjoy the moment, for she sensed an opportunity.

'Cup of tea, Walt?' she asked, as she pushed herself to her feet.

'M-m?'

'Cup of tea?' she repeated.

'Oh! No. Thank you,' he dismissed; the perfect answer as all Amanda really wanted was to head back towards the house.

She moved unnoticed past Christian, who was gradually restoring his vehicle's shine. It was a top of the line Wagoneer and judging by the delicate way he touched the vehicle, it was incredibly dear to him. Amanda quietly opened the front door and entered the house. She followed the sound of movement and ducked into the drawing room as Karen led the children down the staircase to the toy cupboard. Inside were a host of communal toys such as baby dolls, skipping ropes, marbles, conkers, chalk, crayons, the chess board, various other wooden playing boards with sets of balls and a bright red fire engine. Karen pulled on a chord and a naked light bulb sparked to life.

'Reuben,' said Karen, summoning him forward and allowing him to enter the cupboard to select a toy. He opted for the fire engine and walked back out in excitement.

'Gordon,' she said, like a militant leader commanding her troops.

'I wanna play chess with Georgina,' he declared, which came as no surprise.

'Not today. Pick something else,' she instructed.

'Chess. Yah. I definitely wanna play chess,' he repeated.

She lowered her body and spoke slowly, her inner venom working its way through the throbbing veins that appeared on her pale neck.

'Choose-something-else!' she snarled.

'Yah,' said Gordon, stepping into the room and looking around. Again, his head only seemed to shift between two key positions, but something about his manner suggested he was absorbing all of the information around him.

'Yah,' he considered. 'Yah. Okay. I wanna play follows.'

Knowing Karen would be occupied for a while, Amanda finally had the perfect opportunity to spend a little time alone with Christian – something that had seemed surprisingly difficult throughout her stay. Never did she feel more alive than when she was playing detective and the adrenalin overtook the emotions she felt regarding her potential pregnancy.

By the time she walked back outside, the top half of Christian's body had disappeared under his jeep and a set of tools had been placed next to his water bucket.

That's a mighty thorough clean! thought Amanda.

'I just bumped into Karen,' she said, winning his attention.

Christian pulled himself out into view and looked up at her.

'Don't worry. It happens to us all!' he jested.

He was never too busy to fire a flirtatious smile her way, something she had played up to since their first encounter.

'Seemed like she was on the warpath about something,' prodded Amanda in an initial attempt to goad information from him.

'She'll be okay,' he replied.

Amanda nodded.

H-m… maybe a change of tactic.

'Your jeep's in quite a state. You do some damage to it?' she asked.

'Yeah. The dirt tracks around here are crazy,' he replied, grabbing hold of a spanner before disappearing under the vehicle again.

'Did I hear you go out last night?' she ventured.

She noticed his body become still for a moment.

'Yeah. I tried to leave quietly,' he assured her.

Didn't you just? She wanted to say, in relation to the fact he'd let his car coast down most of the hill in darkness. It was, however, feasible that his actions were simply an act of courtesy.

'Oh! It's okay. It was late, though,' she remarked.

'I have trouble sleeping. Sometimes a drive helps.'

Oh really? In your hunting gear?

'Like insomnia?' asked Amanda.

'Exactly!' said Christian, who slid back out from under the jeep to grab hold of his jack. He placed the device on the ground next to the back wheel and, for the first time, he seemed to be avoiding eye contact.

'Did it start when your wife died?'

'You ask a lot of questions,' he said, in a way that insinuated he wanted no more.

'I know. Forgive me, it's just… I'd like to know more about you. Not that I have a right to or anything. I mean, you can tell me to get lost or whatev—'

'Without my wife, my dreams are over,' he blurted, in a moment of honesty that took them both by surprise.

Amanda fell silent as Christian used a cloth to wipe smudges of oil from his arms and hands. His face was a picture of distant regret.

'And without dreams, I guess there's no need to sleep, right?' he continued, his eyes beginning to water.

She stepped towards him. Ever so subtly, he recoiled. It was enough to let her know he didn't wish to be held, yet he still seemed receptive to her sympathies.

'Hey! It's okay,' said Amanda, softly. 'I know how it feels to lose someone.'

*

Back across the yard, Georgina and Gordon had angled a large plank of wood from the bench to the ground and were playing fondly under Karen's supervision, whose face seemed likely to cave at the sight of the children's joy.

'Roll the boss, Gord,' prompted Georgina.

'Yah!'

His arm shot out and he rolled an iron ball down the plank, which soon thudded onto the ground.

'Where is it?' asked Georgina.

'Down the bottom. To the left,' he informed her.

'The left?'

'Yah. On the left. Down the bottom. You go first. Sunday 13th February, 1972. Georgina's go. Knuckle-down.'

Georgina, armed with a dusty white ball, prepared to roll it down the plank – the object of the game being to get the most number of balls closest to the "boss" ball after each player had rolled three times.

Karen's scowl worsened as she nudged Walter. He looked up from his paper and she nodded towards the car park, where Amanda and Christian were locked in a tender embrace. It was an image that made Karen's blood boil. Whatever Amanda's reasons for getting close to Christian, she was enraging the most ruthless of enemies.

CHAPTER NINE

The Boy from Room Four
Sunday 13th February, 1972

Amanda was undoubtedly making progress with her investigation, but as she helped Margaret prepare dinner her eyes continued to wander back to the kitchen clock that ticked away relentlessly on the wall. She could not escape the fact she was running out of time and if she was going to be satisfied she'd done all she could, she would have to be more aggressive in her approach.

'Maggie, where's David?' she asked.

Margaret, in the midst of peeling potatoes, hesitated – only for the slightest moment, but enough to let Amanda know the question made her feel uneasy.

'I'm sorry dear?' she said, clearly buying herself a little more thinking time.

'David. The boy from room four. You showed me his bedroom but I haven't met him yet,' she queried.

'Oh yes. Of course! Young David,' said Margaret, trying to disguise her discomfort. 'He's being disciplined,' she eventually revealed.

'Disciplined?'

'Yes. By Christian.'

'Disciplined how?' asked Amanda, sensing that she wouldn't like the answer.

'The usual. Time in the isolation room,' Margaret informed her, smacking her lips together as though her mouth was dry.

'The isolation room?' Amanda repeated, judgingly. 'Is that on the top floor?'

'That's right, dear,' Margaret confirmed.

'Maggie, I've been here since Friday! The boy's been left alone for all this time?'

'Well… I go and talk to him when I can, but Christian thinks it's best he be left alone to think about what he did,' revealed

Margaret.

'And what did he do, exactly?'

'He tried to glue the doors shut and burn the house down when we were all sleeping.'

The answer was definitely more extreme than Amanda had expected. If it was true – and she had no reason to disbelieve Margaret – then the act was both shocking and malicious. Though quite why a young boy would behave in such a way was the main point of interest.

'Don't be too alarmed,' said Margaret, responding to Amanda's silence. 'He's a lovely boy. He just needs to be watched closely. He suffers from bouts of paranoia, you see.'

Amanda had read about paranoia in one of her books. It was often the cause of many extreme acts and many experts agreed that those who suffered from such psychological burdens were a significant danger within society because they were so incredibly unpredictable. One leading doctor from the States concluded that the key to crime prevention was in identifying the increasing frequency and severity of the person's impulses as it was never a case of *if* such people committed heinous crimes, but *when*.

'How often does he act like that?' asked Amanda.

'Sometimes he says he sees things; horrific things! We keep telling him it's all in his head, but he won't have it. He accuses everyone of being against him and gets himself in a right state. Walt thinks he may be schizophrenic,' Margaret told her.

'Walter isn't qualified to make such judgements,' Amanda seethed, becoming increasingly frustrated at the liberties they each appeared to be taking with a boy who was in clear and desperate need of help. 'You know what? This is bullshit!'

'I'm sorry?' said Margaret, taken aback and unsure of how to react to Amanda's sudden assertion.

'Give me the key to the attic,' Amanda demanded of her.

Feeling pressured, Margaret hesitated.

'I can't, my lovely.'

'Give me the key to the isolation room. *Please*!' asked Amanda, replacing her aggression with a tone that implied she only wanted to help.

'Sweetie, I can't. I don't have it,' Margaret informed her.

'Then who does?'

Based on what Margaret had already said, Amanda assumed the person that held the key would be Christian. She was right. Had it have been Karen that was responsible for the boy's misery then it would have made a lot more sense, but that Christian – a seemingly carefree and charming man – was capable of such sinister, dated behaviour without showing a shred of empathy was somehow more disturbing. To Amanda, it was evidence she could trust nothing she had seen so far within the home. She needed to see the boy and if confronting the homeowner was the only way to achieve that, then so be it.

*

'No. Now's not a good time,' Christian said into the telephone.

'Well, you said you wanted me to get my best guy and I got him,' said a gruff voice on the other end of the line.

'I appreciate that, but like I said, it's a delicate time,' repeated Christian, authoritatively.

Calling from a payphone in town was a rugged man named Andy. Many of the locals were afraid of Andy as he was feisty and never shied away from a fight. This didn't bother Christian, though. In fact, the Christian that dealt with Andy so sternly cut a very different figure to the man that was often so playful around Amanda.

He looked up to the locked office door as it was tested from the other side. Frustrated, Amanda banged hard from the hallway.

'Christian, it's, Amanda. I'd like to speak with you, please.'

'I'll call you back,' Christian said to Andy, hanging up before awaiting a response.

As Christian opened the door, Amanda looked sour and his mother flustered as she squirmed in the background. He monitored the pair of them with intrigue.

'Can I help?' he asked.

'Yes. I'd like the key to the isolation room,' said Amanda, bluntly.

'Why's that?' asked Christian, calmly.

'He's been locked in there for far too long! That's why!' she

68

simmered.

'Look…' began Christian, slinking back into his office as he arranged loose pieces of paper into a pile. 'I appreciate your concern, but we have certain rules here. The children know where they stand with those rules and we can't just change them without warning. It'll confuse them,' he claimed.

'That's very thoughtful of you but I feel confusion is probably less damaging than isolation,' retorted Amanda, with a boldness that threatened to shed her false skin.

Christian took a moment to gauge her and suddenly Amanda became aware she had revealed a significant part of her true self. The exposure made her feel momentarily vulnerable.

'This conversation is over,' said Christian, reclaiming the seat at his desk and looking down at the paperwork he had assembled like a newsreader playing up for the cameras during the closing credits.

However, Amanda persevered, stepping into his office without permission – a simple act that seemed to irk Christian and worry Margaret greatly. She knew how particular her son was with his rules and feared Amanda would soon cross a line from which she would be unable to return.

'Amanda love…' she tried to interject, but Amanda's cards were brazenly on the table.

For her, it was time to raise the stakes.

'You know what? You were honest with me today so I'm going to be honest with you,' Amanda began. 'When I was young, my stepfather raped me. Repeatedly. Over and over again for almost three years. My mum stayed with him the whole time and when I tried to tell her, she didn't…'

Amanda fought to stay focused amidst her emotions.

'She didn't believe me,' she eventually added. 'Looking back now, do you know who I blame for everything? I blame her. Not the man who touched me in ways he never should have; not the man who grossly took advantage of a helpless child, but my own mother, because *she* had the power to stop it and she chose not to.'

Amanda took a further step towards Christian's desk as she locked her sorrow-filled eyes onto his.

'Christian, the children in this house don't need to be condemned. They can still live a happy life, but when David grows up, he'll remember that you had the power to help him. He's just a boy,' she said, softly.

Suddenly, Karen marched towards the open office door.

'What's going on here?' she spat, incensed at her exclusion.

'Just a minute!' said Christian, dismissing her as he considered Amanda's plea.

He looked towards his mother, who stared straight back at him. 'Do you trust me?' he asked of Amanda.

It was not the response she was expecting.

'What kind of question's that?' she hesitated. 'I hardly know you.'

'But do you *trust* me?' he asked again, with a little more intensity. 'I am the homeowner. It's my name on the wall. I wanted you to work here because, out of all the applicants, you were by far the best suited to this home. I chose you because I felt you would understand why we do things differently here.'

'All I'm saying is…'

'Please!' interrupted Christian. 'I have listened to you, and now I ask that you listen to me. You need to make a decision right now. Either you leave the home, with no hard feelings, and return to your life in the city, or you stay here. If you stay, I assure you, you will learn precisely why these rules are in place. This is your choice to make and yours alone, but today, right now, I *cannot* release David from the room. Nor can I let you inside.'

Amanda looked down. Her colleagues probably thought she was looking at the floor, but she was looking towards her belly, where she believed her own child lay. It was Sunday. The day she had promised to return home. Tony would be expecting her in the office that evening to report her findings, but she knew that when she saw her man, it would not be the story of the care home that would take precedent. Instead, it would be her turn to act in an uncharacteristically sentimental way. She would tell him that she loved him completely. She would inform him that she was carrying his baby and then they would go to bed and make love. It would be the beginning of their new life together; a future that had been destined all along.

Amanda had visited the home and stayed for three days as intended, and despite learning of some unorthodox methods, there was no stonewall evidence that the abuse the children had suffered came from the carers. Christian had given her the out she needed to walk away without suspicion... but there was something about the way he had just spoken.

"If you stay, I assure you, you will learn precisely why these rules are in place."

Whatever did that mean? It was the most peculiar way he could have phrased it and, as with so many other facts regarding the home, she felt there was something just beneath the surface that, if she scratched just a little deeper, could lead to something of real significance.

She loved Tony. She knew that now and if she was true to him their love would last a lifetime. Therefore, what harm could a couple more days do?

'I don't care if it happens inside or outside of that room, but I want to meet David tomorrow. I've told you my reasons. Promise me that and I'll stay,' Amanda bargained.

Karen scoffed in the background.

Margaret frowned at Karen's reaction as she held onto the hope Amanda had done enough to bring her son to his senses. As a silence ensued, Karen's smug expression morphed into one of discomfort.

'You can't be considering this?' Karen hissed.

'Would you just be quiet?' said Christian, shedding a little of his own false skin.

He looked back to Amanda and offered a hearty smile.

'I promise. Tomorrow you can meet David.'

CHAPTER TEN

Testing Borders

Sunday 13th February, 1972

Amanda waltzed around the kitchen, adding creative touches to dinner as though she had been there for many years. Suddenly, she felt optimistic about her efforts making a difference towards the children within the house. No longer was Margaret the only one who lightened their mood. Instead, it had become a burden both women shared and this was a reality in which they revelled.

She pulled a block of cheese out of the fridge and then flipped open a couple of cupboards to retrieve a small grater and a large oven-proof dish. Tonight, she would make her special cauliflower cheese to accompany the roast chicken dinner both she and Margaret were preparing. Amanda had learnt how to cook when she was young on account of largely having to look after herself, but she never thought she'd enjoy the kitchen as much as she did at that moment. She looked up to notice Margaret staring at her; her usual grin replaced with a sullen expression.

'What's wrong?' asked Amanda.

'Amanda Connors. Black hair. Light frame. Green eyes. Abusive father. Neglectful mother. Determined spirit. I knew I'd met you before.'

It was inevitable. Margaret had finally remembered her from Saint Matthews care home. Amanda's initial reaction was to feel bad about saying she'd never heard of the place. If it wasn't for Saint Matthews, and Margaret in particular, working so hard to stabilise her traumatic childhood, Amanda dreaded to think what would have happened to her. Denying the place was one thing, but telling an outright lie to Margaret was quite another.

'Maggie, I...'

As far as Margaret was concerned, there was no need for words. Instead, she stepped towards Amanda and pulled her into a hug. Amanda chuckled at first, awkwardly patting the woman on the back. She expected the moment to soon pass, but it didn't. Margaret pulled her tighter, making it clear she wouldn't settle for a half-hearted embrace. Eventually, Amanda's resistance fell and she held Margaret equally as tight.

'What a fine, fine woman you grew up to be. I'm so proud of you,' Margaret whispered sweetly. 'Everybody at Saint Matthews would be, too.'

Her kind words took Amanda by surprise and somewhere deep down, they resonated. Suddenly, Amanda was the one who was clutching the tightest.

Right on cue, Karen entered in the midst of her candle-lighting routine. She frowned upon the alien behaviour taking place before her in a desperate attempt to belittle the moment, but it didn't work. The two women continued the embrace and it was Karen who felt out of place by the time she quitted the room. On their own terms, Margaret and Amanda pulled away from one another, exchanging looks of genuine respect as they each ensured the other was okay. Tearful but happy, they moved around the room smiling as they continued their work in therapeutic silence.

*

At the dinner table, the feeling that anything was possible continued to stimulate Amanda as she monitored the other residents' behaviour closely. With the exception of David, Ellie and the groundskeeper, whom Amanda had yet to encounter, they were all in attendance. Margaret spoon-fed Malcolm having mashed his dinner up into a paste, making it easier to digest; Walter helped Gordon by cutting his food into small pieces; Christian watched over Georgina as they both enjoyed their meal and upon looking at Reuben, who was sat staring at Amanda, she playfully poked her tongue out at him. He didn't expect it and was forced into a slow, secret smile. Indeed, Karen was the only carer neglecting to actually show care for anyone around her as she ate in stony silence. She didn't acknowledge a soul, including her doting husband. All in all, things had taken shape quite nicely, but Amanda felt there was still progress to be made before the day was through.

'What are we going to do about Ellie?' she asked.

'Oh, I'll take her dinner up when I'm done,' answered Christian, casually, politely covering his mouth with a napkin as he spoke.

'I was talking more about the fact she doesn't really interact with anyone.'

As if by magic, her words had managed to steal Karen's attention.

'We each see Ellie every day,' added Walter, just to make sure she knew that was the case.

'That's great! As you should, but that's up in her room, right? She's holed up with barely any daylight. It's not good for her,' said Amanda.

'Alright. That's it!' snapped Karen. 'I've had enough of your interference! We've run this home a good many years before you got here and we'll continue to do so long after you've gone. These children are sick and they need routine,' she insisted.

'I agree, but some of the *routines* you provide would be better suited in a prison,' quipped Amanda, adopting the same kind of laidback demeanour she'd seen Christian use when winding her up so effectively.

'Are you going to sit there and listen to this?' Karen asked of Christian.

Amanda found it odd that she would always look to him for support as opposed to her husband.

Christian thought for a moment as he calmly chewed on his food. He crossed the cutlery on his plate and placed his elbows on the table as he interlinked his fingers, peering at Amanda over the top of his clasped hands.

'What would you propose we do?' he asked her.

'I didn't mean reason with her!' Karen seethed.

'If you don't mind, I'd like to hear her thoughts. I'm sure she means well but, by the same token, she may not realise the severity of Ellie's condition, so I'm happy to talk this through,' he insisted.

'This is outrageous!' spat Karen as she squirmed in her chair.

Yet another stage had been set on which Amanda intended to shine.

'You're quite right. I don't know everything about Ellie yet, but

I've been here for three days now and seen her only once and spending so much time alone, especially when vulnerable, *cannot* be helping. The same goes for David,' she added.

'Now she's a psychologist!' Karen mocked.

Amanda knew that Karen's impatience was a sign she was winning, so she ignored her petty comments and explained herself collectedly, focusing all of her attention on Christian.

'All I ask is to spend more time with them both so I can integrate them better with the other children. It will help,' she assured him, feeling absolutely convinced herself.

'I have no problem with that,' admitted Christian. 'But my primary concern is safety, so I want you to spend time alone with Ellie in her room until you're sure you can handle her around the others. Agreed?'

As Christian spoke, Amanda had noted the reactions of everybody around the table. It was clear they couldn't quite believe what they were hearing. In a place so regimented, rules didn't simply change at the drop of a hat, yet there he was agreeing to almost anything Amanda requested. He would add his own set of conditions, but all the same, Amanda had to give him credit. He was hard but fair and that was cause for great optimism. In the faces of Margaret and the children, Amanda could sense her own inner joy was shared by those that mattered.

'Excellent!' Amanda beamed. 'I'll start by taking Ellie her dinner.'

*

The verbal agreement to spend some one-on-one time with Ellie was a significant step in the right direction, but as Amanda approached the girl's bedroom and fumbled for key number 5, her mind told her that winning Ellie's acceptance would be another battle entirely. In one hand, she balanced a tray that held a plastic plate, plastic cutlery and an apple. She had been told that plastics had to be used with Ellie at all times due to her attempts at suicide and these utensils were only allowed whilst Ellie was in the company of an adult.

Upon reaching door 5, Amanda was sharply reminded of their last encounter. She observed the hand that held the tray. It was shaking. Not until that moment did Amanda realise she was genuinely afraid. However, getting Ellie onside was a key part of her plan and so without delaying any further, she took a deep breath and unlocked the door. She darted inside and placed the tray on the floor before Ellie had time to register her presence. As suspected, she wasn't best pleased to see Amanda, who was little more than a stranger to her. Ellie jumped up from her bed and charged at the intruder, but now that Amanda knew what to expect, the struggle that ensued wasn't quite so daunting and she dealt with the situation far more easily, manoeuvring Ellie into a grip where, despite her impressive strength and determination, she was unable to cause any damage. Amanda closed her eyes and started to count. It was one hundred and eighteen seconds before Ellie's rage subsided. Little-by-little, Amanda released her grip, tightening it again immediately when Ellie's aggression rose, teaching the youngster that her freedom came at the price of calmness. Like a dog whose trainer tightened a lead around its neck whenever it did wrong, Ellie soon learnt that she would be afforded her space if only she relaxed.

Once free, Ellie ran back over to her bed, curling up into a foetal position with her back to Amanda and her hands covering her ears. Her body language suggested she felt hard done by. Amanda monitored her for several minutes and gathered that the girl merely felt frustrated – completely understandable given that she had been treated like a prisoner.

Amanda sat patiently with her back against the wall and the plate of food lying on the floor between them. On her first visit to the room, she hadn't noticed a small bowl on the floor that appeared to be her toilet. Maybe it was empty last time, but right now the half-filled bowl of urine stank up the place. It had been partially spilled in the tussle and the smell made the silence seem eternal.

'You have a beautiful name!' said Amanda, desperate to begin a conversation.

As a child, particularly a child in the custody of various homes and foster parents, Amanda had been in front of endless adults trying to negotiate a way to win her trust. It was the sincere way that her own favourite artificial mother had complimented her name that led Amanda to often use this as her opening line when talking to children.

'I knew a girl called Ellie when I was at school. She was my best friend,' she continued.

Amanda did not expect a response but she knew the girl could do nothing but listen. Therefore, she reasoned that if she was nice enough, Ellie would drop her defences eventually. The girl simply wasn't used to company and so couldn't be blamed for her lack of social skills or her vacant desire to improve them.

'I'd like to take you out into the garden soon. You could play with the others. Would you like that?' asked Amanda.

Still there was no answer, but Amanda persevered. She spoke niceties and informed the girl of general things such as what the weather was like and what the other kids had been up to.

'Dinner's good today. I know because I helped make it,' she said with a smile.

It was Ellie's determination not to eat that led Amanda to feel defeated. As she had to take all the utensils with her, all she could do was leave the apple, which she desperately hoped the girl would eat, for what could she do if Ellie continued to reject the food? It didn't even bear thinking about. All she could do was let the girl know she was in no way a threat, be kind and ensure her she would be back very soon, but in her mind she ran through possible tactics that might speed up the process of winning Ellie's trust.

As Amanda gently closed and locked Ellie's door, her bubble had been well and truly burst. She wasn't untouchable, after all. She couldn't even make a starving girl eat nice food! At that moment, however, she realised she had inadvertently provided herself with an opportunity to explore the door to the isolation room. She peered down the hall to make sure nobody else was coming and then, at long last, crept silently along the narrow, pitch black corridor and up the stairs until she was able to place her hands on the door. She tapped on it gently.

'Hello? Hello... David?' she whispered. 'David!' she repeated, this time a little louder.

She put her ear to the door and listened. She wasn't to know how dark the room was inside, nor that the darkness magnified every single sound she made, serving only to frighten the young boy. If she could have seen him and the conditions he was being kept in, she would have tore the door down with her bare hands, for at the end of the isolation chamber, underneath a solitary window that angled the moonlight into the attic, young David Newsome stood hunched over – tired, hungry and terrified. Old rusty chains kept him upright, precisely as they had been fashioned to do.

'Psssst! David!' Amanda whispered once more.

It's no good. She thought. *He won't talk until he sees me. I'll take care of that tomorrow.*

Resigned to her second crushing setback within just as many minutes, she walked away, oblivious to the boy's helpless, lonely sobs on the other side of the door.

*

Amanda returned to the kitchen and quickly scraped Ellie's untouched dinner into the bin so that Karen wouldn't see it and latch onto her failure. She then worked hard to hide her disappointment before re-entering the dining room, where the residents were finishing off their meal. The silence, coupled with the expressions on everybody's faces – Karen's reddened cheeks and the sheepish uncertainty of the children – made it clear that tensions had been running high in her absence.

'I hope it went well,' said Karen, unable to hide her bitterness.

'Very well, thank you,' Amanda replied, feigning total satisfaction.

If there was one thing Amanda hated, it was being goaded. It created a rush of blood to her head that often led her into irrational actions and without even thinking it through, she thought of another way to get at Karen.

'Oh! I'd like to take Malcolm into town tomorrow, if you don't mind?' she blurted.

'What?' screeched Karen, irately.

'What would you do when you got there?' asked Christian.

'I don't know. I haven't been there myself yet and I'd like to know my way around. With your permission, I'd like to take him,' Amanda replied.

'It's completely unnecessary. He wouldn't take anything in,' Karen dismissed.

'That's your opinion, but I happen to think the occasional trip may be useful. It certainly wouldn't do any harm,' Amanda countered.

'Go to town. Yah! I'd like to go to town. Haven't been there for 464 days. 464,' Gordon muttered.

'Well, maybe if tomorrow goes well, I can take you next time, Gord. And then you, Georgina! What do you think about that?' she asked the young girl.

It wasn't often that an adult asked a question of a child within the house, and a subtle smile graced Georgina's face as she considered the possibility.

'Yah! I'd like to go. Me and Georgina would definitely like to go town,' Gordon continued.

'I'm sure Walter would be happy to take us. You do go there to get your morning papers, after all,' Amanda prodded.

Everybody's eyes landed on Walter, but it was Karen's gaze he felt most of all, her piercing stare burning through his skin like acid.

'H-m,' he grunted, resisting the urge to get too heavily involved.

'I wanna go town!' added Reuben.

'Of course, Reuben! We wouldn't leave you out,' Amanda assured him.

'Yah, 464 days,' Gordon reminded them.

'Can we go?' asked an excited Georgina. 'Can we?'

Margaret attempted to hide her delight as the scene unfolded around the table. Christian suddenly felt the pressure from all angles.

'You don't have to decide now. Please, talk it through while I do the dishes,' said Amanda, who gathered some plates, looked defiantly into Karen's eyes and then stepped victoriously out of the room.

CHAPTER ELEVEN

Serpent's Kiss

Sunday 13ᵗʰ February, 1972

It had been a long day and nobody had felt the strain more than Christian, who sat drinking his favourite whiskey in his office. He loved his space and often found he was most comfortable in his own company. The fact he so revered privacy could partially explain how he found it so easy to turn his back on the outside world and move his family to Exmoor.

On a nearby record player, Jonny Cash's *Ring of Fire* played quietly as Christian studied an old photograph of himself with his parents. The picture captured what was a much happier time. Within the frozen image, Christian practically glowed with optimism, Margaret brimmed with happiness and Stanley, with his hands wrapped lovingly around both of them, wore a huge grin of content.

Christian smiled as he stared at the image of his father, becoming lost in a series of rarely visited memories; memories that soon made the smile fade. So invested was Christian in his mind's offerings that it took him a few moments to respond to the gentle knock at the door. When he answered, he was unsurprised to see Amanda, who on this occasion waited for an invite before stepping into his office. Just before she entered, she noticed Karen watching from the shadows but acted as though she hadn't.

'I'm sorry to bother you again,' said Amanda. 'I know you're probably busy.'

'Oh yeah! Busy getting through this,' he joked, raising his glass as if toasting her before taking another swig of his drink. 'What do you need?'

'Well, I really just wanted to say I'm sorry if I've upset Karen. I don't want to step on anyone's toes here, but I really do feel there are things I'd like to explore.'

'I think we get that,' he replied.

Unsure of how to take his mood, Amanda fell into an awkward

silence.

'It's fine!' insisted Christian. 'Like I said, if I believe your ideas have credence, I'll support you any way I can.'

Amanda smiled. It was just the kind of response she was after.

'Great!' she said, encouraged by his support.

She hesitated for a moment before glancing towards the phone that sat on his desk.

'Is there anything else?' he asked, noticing she was in no hurry to leave.

'Umm... I wondered if I could use your phone?'

'Of course!' he said, pointing to it with an open palm. 'It's here any time you need it.'

Amanda stalled for a moment to see if he would excuse himself. Instead, he headed over to the record player and sifted through his vinyl collection, making it clear she would have to deal with him being in the room. Slowly, she sat on the chair trying to think of the best way to approach her conversation with Tony as she dialled the number to the editorial office. As the phone rang, Christian poured himself another short, leaning against the large wooden unit on which the record player stood. He chose the song *She's Not There* by The Zombies and closed his eyes as it played. He looked like a man actively trying to unwind, but it was an aim that proved difficult. On his neck, Amanda saw the string necklace on which she knew the claw was attached.

Odd that he should wear it without his hunting gear. She thought.

Suddenly, Tony answered, stealing her focus away.

'Hello?' he asked, somewhat gruffly.

'Oh! Hi! It's me,' she replied, astutely aware that Christian could hear everything she said.

'Where are you? You're supposed to be here already!' he reminded her, sounding agitated.

'Yeah. I'm very well, thank you. How are things at home?'

The warmth of Amanda's voice was in stark contrast to the worry in Tony's, but he was savvy. He could tell by the way she spoke that somebody was listening and that could only mean one thing. She was still at the home.

'You promised me you'd leave!' he hissed, under his breath.

'I'm sorry, Dad. I just... it's been so busy here that I've only just had the chance to call.'

Dad? Where did that come from?

Ever since her departure, Tony had been craving to see her, hear her voice and hold her. He had scarcely eaten and had been counting the minutes until she returned so he could make sure everything was alright between them, and there he was dealing with the crushing fact she would not be coming home, forcing the torture to continue. For Amanda, all she wanted was to tell him the great news; that she loved him, she missed him and she believed she was carrying his child, but all of those emotions had to be swallowed.

Tony took a breath and tried to clear his head.

'Just let me know you're okay,' he said.

She looked up towards Christian, who still had his eyes closed, his body swaying to the music.

'Yes,' she replied.

'And if you're still there, you obviously still believe there's a story?'

'M-m, h-m,' she confirmed.

'How much longer do you need?' asked Tony.

'A few days,' she speculated.

'A few? No,' he said, assertively. 'Tuesday night you'll be back here. And I mean *here*! Not a phone call. Whatever you have on them by then, we use, but if you have nothing, we assume there *is* nothing. Understand?'

'Of course!' she agreed, with added enthusiasm.

There was a short silence on the phone as both Tony and Amanda sat stuck in their own conflicting sadness.

'It's nice to talk to you,' Tony finally admitted.

'You too,' she said. 'I love you!'

With that, Amanda put the phone down. She looked back to Christian, who finally opened his eyes, and smiled appreciatively.

'Thank you,' she said, before pushing herself to her feet.

'No problem,' he insisted.

As Amanda readied herself to leave, she saw a framed photograph hanging behind Christian's desk in which he caressed a woman's belly.

Lydia! She thought, suddenly becoming aware this was the only pictorial evidence she had seen of his wife within the house. The pregnant couple appeared the epitome of happiness.

82

'Are you alright?' asked Christian, snapping Amanda out of her daze.

'Oh! Yeah. I just… stood up too fast! I'll see you in the morning,' she said, leaving the room with haste.

'She was pregnant!' exclaimed Amanda into her Dictaphone as she paced around the room. 'This means Christian must have lost them both! It finally explains why both families came here. They were bonded through trauma. It makes sense now why Maggie didn't want to talk about it. It was a tragedy that must have broken their hearts. I have to say, there are many things I don't like about their methods, on which a full report will follow, but I believe when both families moved here, their intentions may have been good.'

She switched the Dictaphone off, continuing to think over what she had just learnt. She placed her hand on her belly and felt incredibly lucky. To have lost a child must have been awful, but for the family to lose the mother as well. Well, it must have been almost too much to bear. Suddenly, Amanda felt a pang of guilt about having come into their home in order to analyse their lives; lives that were tinged with unfathomable tragedy.

In Christian's office, the needle no longer touched the record. Instead, it hovered in mid-air, bobbing amidst the gentle hissing sound of the vinyl as it went round and round. Christian sat still in his chair, his eyes were red but he was wide awake.

'I see the way you look at her,' said Karen, who prowled around him somewhat menacingly.

'You do? And how's that?' he asked, despondently.

'You know exactly what I mean,' she said. 'You used to look at me like that.'

A sudden sadness washed over Karen's face as she found it within herself to be vulnerable. Very few people had seen her in such a way. Indeed, when Walter first courted her, it was a very singular combination of traits that had won his affections. She was fierce and unafraid to speak her mind. She had strong morals and acted with conviction. However, during the moments they shared alone together, she would reveal a soft and loving nature. That Walter was the only one to see her true self made their relationship all the more special to him. Life, however, had a very uncanny knack of changing things.

Standing by helplessly as cancer ate away at her mother changed Karen. Suddenly, the glimpses of beauty that had appeared in the world became harder to find, as did her God, who never answered a single one of her prayers as she pleaded for her mother to be spared her humiliation and pain. The disease took a heavier toll on Karen's father, who never recovered from watching his wife's demise. The man, renowned for being eternally cheerful, became a shadow of his former self. Within three months of his wife's funeral, he wilted away like a broken flower, dying through what Karen believed to be a broken heart.

Time did not prove to be a healer as so many people claimed and in one fell swoop, Walter lost his mother, father and beloved younger sister when an over-tired lorry driver fell asleep at the wheel and ploughed straight into their car as they journeyed up to the Lake District. Walter's sister had talked about her wedding day ever since she was eight-years-old and when she finally met the man of her dreams she was desperate to introduce him to her parents. The Scot, who came from Aberdeen, had arranged for his immediate family to spend the weekend at a holiday home with her parents. The only reason Walter was not in the car was because he had already met and approved of her fiancé during an impromptu trip to Oxford, where he was working as a butler. The fatal accident achieved two things: it led Walter to ask for Karen's hand in marriage so that he might live out his sister's dream of creating a glorious white wedding, but although she accepted, it pushed Karen further into her belief that the world was a bad place where only awful things happened.

One day, shortly after their wedding, Walter found a small notebook lying on the kitchen table of their home. He opened it out of gentle curiosity and what he found disturbed him greatly. Through a series of manic scribblings, Karen had vented her inner anger, describing how she felt the fire of hell growing inside her, burning her insides and leaving her dead to the world. She noted how everything around her had lost its innocence and that, in hating herself to the point she no longer wished to live, she could find nothing but hatred for others and could not abide their happiness. Walter returned the book to the table and never spoke of his findings. Instead, he kept a close eye on his wife and took painstaking efforts to pull her out of her depressed state. One day, quite by accident, Karen fell pregnant and for a while it seemed to have returned her zest for life. However, this was to prove a temporary relief, and mothering her own children would eventually provide the final push towards bitter and twisted delusions that spiralled out of all control.

*

'I won't have this conversation,' said Christian, adamantly. 'What we did was wrong,' he added, simmering with regret.

It was not a rejection Karen was prepared to take and, moving towards him like a ravenous snake, she wrapped herself around him and kissed him on the mouth. Christian pushed her away, his face distorted as though he'd swallowed poison.

'What are you doing?' he yelled. 'I told you *never* again!'

'Lydia left us, Christian. *She* left *us!* Remember that,' she spat, angrily, before slithering back into the darkness of the downstairs hallway.

CHAPTER TWELVE

A Promise is a Promise

Monday 14th February, 1972

Breakfast was in full flow as Margaret arranged the children at the dining room table and Amanda added her own special touches in the kitchen. She had cut the toast into small triangles instead of chunky rectangles and by using a small knife she had managed to turn the tomatoes into decorative food that the children suddenly wanted to eat. Margaret smiled broadly at Amanda, who hummed lightly as she placed the appetising meals in front of Malcolm and Gordon, leaving Reuben drooling in wait.

'Feeling at home now, are we?' she remarked.

'I am,' grinned Amanda.

'Good morning, Amanda,' said Georgina happily as she stepped into the kitchen.

'Good morning to you, Georgie,' she replied. 'Take your seat. Yours is coming right up!'

'Is there anything I can do?' Margaret asked as Amanda made her way back to the door.

'Sure! You can bring in the rest of the plates while I take Ellie her breakfast.'

*

The thought of entering Ellie's room no longer held any fear for Amanda now that she knew she could handle it alone. She slipped into the room, quickly placing the tray back onto the floor as she prepared to restrain her. On this occasion, however, Ellie simply lay on her side like a lioness happy to let its keeper tend to business around her. Amanda noticed that the apple from the previous evening had been lightly nibbled but otherwise abandoned. Its contents were brown and unfit for consumption.

Damn it!

'I cooked most of this today,' enthused Amanda. 'Why don't you try it? You must be starving!'

As she expected, Ellie ignored her, but the fact she had not launched an attack marked definite progress. Amanda picked the plate up from the floor, along with its plastic utensils, and stepped closer.

'Look at the tomatoes!' she said, as though it were the most exciting thing in the world.

Ellie didn't move and so Amanda walked to the other side of the bed and held the plate directly in front of her. Ellie observed the food briefly before rolling over. Amanda shrugged and walked back to the other side of the bed.

'Ever played with marbles?' she asked, completely out of the blue. 'It's a shame you don't have any because we could play together.'

Amanda placed her hand in her pocket and pulled out an elaborate marble that had vibrant colours running through it, like a rainbow trapped in the glass. She had seen a whole stack of them under the stairs when helping pack the toys away and hoped she may be able to use them as a bargaining tool. She appeared to be right as the mere sight of it improved Ellie's interest in her significantly.

'This is one of my favourites but I have hundreds. Would you like it?' she asked, tantalisingly waving it in front of the girl. Suddenly, Ellie tried to take it but Amanda closed her hand and pulled it away.

'Nuh-uh,' she said, shaking her head. 'If you want it, you have to earn it. I tell you what. Every time you answer a question or eat your food, I'll give you a marble. Then, before you know it, you'll have enough marbles to play with.'

Ellie tried to hide her excitement, but the way her eyes suddenly sparkled made it clear Amanda had won her full attention.

'I want to talk about the marks on your arm. How did you get them?'

Suddenly, Ellie slumped back into a sullen look.

'I can't give you a marble unless you answer me. Did you do it to yourself?'

The girl didn't much move, but Amanda could tell her mind was a flurry of activity and she developed high hopes that Ellie would soon talk to her.

'You wouldn't understand,' Ellie eventually replied in a deflated, barely audible voice.

'Why don't you try me?' tested Amanda, before being reacquainted with the back of Ellie's head as she rolled over on the bed.

Deep down inside, Amanda was tempted to push harder, but the fact Ellie had finally spoken was significant success for the visit and so Amanda forced herself to ease off. What still troubled her, though, was Ellie's refusal to eat. Her skin was pale and something about the way she was slumped on the bed suggested she didn't have much energy. It suddenly occurred to Amanda that this might even be the reason Ellie didn't attack her… she simply couldn't. Amanda considered her options. She felt that if she left the food then Ellie would have the temptation to eat along with the freedom to do so without feeling like she had "given in" to one of the carers. The risk was that she would have to leave the utensils, something Margaret had specifically told her not to do. Amanda reasoned that if she didn't at least attempt this, though, the girl would soon starve. Also, if blackmailing her with marbles was going to work, she would soon have to trust the girl would not use them to choke herself. Quite simply, a life spent in fear was no life at all, and so Amanda quickly made her decision.

'Ellie, I'm going to leave your food here. I'll be back in a little while,' she said, approaching the door and opening it slightly before turning back.

'I want to help you, Ellie. I hope you can see that,' she said, before leaving the room and locking the door, leaving the youngster to contemplate her words.

*

Feeling productive, Amanda pulled the damp clothes from out of the washing machine and loaded the garments into a wicker basket. She carried it out into the garden where the clothesline stood. Much to her delight, she heard a *snip-snipping* coming from the bottom of the yard where a tall, scruffy figure trimmed a hedge. At long last, after finding countless excuses to linger around his quarters, she had finally laid her eyes on Arthur, the groundskeeper. Without a moment's hesitation, she made her way towards him. Upon noticing this, he nervously shaped to leave.

'Hi! I'm Amanda,' she said, bowling up to him with a smile and an outstretched hand.

At her exuberant greeting, he hesitated.

'Mmm... hallo,' he replied, sounding anxious.

His brow was clammy and he fidgeted considerably. As she took a hold of his hand, she noticed his grip was weak and his palm was sweaty. After a brief, awkward shake, he practically threw her hand back at her.

'You're Arthur, right?' she asked, saying whatever she could think of to keep the conversation going.

'Uh... yah!'

'It's nice to finally meet you,' she said, warmly.

She monitored him closely. His complete lack of confidence prevented him from even making eye contact and he appeared desperate to get away.

'You've done a wonderful job with the garden!' she praised, believing that taking the subject matter and her eye line away from him may afford the man some comfort.

'Th-th-thank you,' he stuttered.

'How come we never see you at the house?'

Just as it seemed Arthur was about to reply, he looked nervously towards the top of the garden where Karen had emerged. She was strutting down towards them and Arthur immediately lowered his head and shied away.

'Amanda, could you give Margaret a hand with the children, please?' she asked in a way that sounded more like an instruction than a request.

'Sure! I'll see you soon, Arthur,' chirped Amanda, offering a kind smile.

He nodded at her and as Amanda took slow steps back towards the house, Karen remained, edging ever closer to him. Amanda stalled for as long as she could but it was clear Karen wouldn't speak until she was out of earshot, so she trotted back up the small grass hill.

'What were you two talking about?' asked Karen.

'N-n-nothing,' dismissed Arthur.

'Nothing, eh?'

He shook his head, assuring her it was true.

'Make sure you keep it that way, you fucking retard!' she snarled, viciously, as she put her face close to his. 'Or you know what will happen. Don't you?'

He whimpered like a dog that had been beaten with a stick.

'Good. Now get back to work!' she demanded, prompting him to fumble for his sheers and continue cutting the hedge, glancing nervously towards her as he did so.

*

Upon entering the house, Amanda revisited Ellie's bedroom where the young girl slept peacefully. Lying on the floor beside the bed was a half empty plate. Amanda could barely contain her joy and the moment made her tearful. She fought hard to keep her emotions in check and moved around the room in silence before picking up the plate. Remaining true to her word, she placed the marble on the floor and left as quietly as she'd entered.

*

As Amanda walked through the first floor hallway, she heard playful noises coming from Reuben and Georgina's bedroom. It was most irregular for the children to be left indoors unattended and so she pushed the door open gently to find Christian sat with him.

'Nee-naw, nee-naw, nee-naw...' Reuben sounded as he pushed the bright red fire engine around on the floor.

Amanda found the boy's enthusiasm infectious and was always pleased to see him happy. When he was playing with toys, particularly his favourite fire engine, he seemed to be in his element, and the sight of Christian playing with him made her feel a little gooey inside. Christian looked up and acknowledged her with a nod.

'You like trucks, don't you Reub?' said Christian.

Reuben nodded his head, too involved in his own world to actually speak.

'Why don't you come outside with the others? It's a beautiful day. It'll be even nicer when the summer gets here, and we've got to make the most of it,' Christian assured him. 'Winter's nearly over. Do you know what comes next?' he asked, encouragingly.

'Schpring!' answered Reuben, to which Amanda smiled.

'That's right!' said Christian, proudly, before ruffling the young boy's hair. 'Come on. Let's walk down with Amanda.'

Reuben looked up in excitement, not having realised she was stood there.

'Where did you come from?' he asked, pushing himself to his feet.

'Ellie's room,' she replied.

Reuben walked over to her, reaching out to hold her hand. She grabbed it happily, balancing Ellie's dirty plate in the other.

'Is she allowed outside?' asked Reuben, innocently

Amanda looked over to Christian.

'Uh... hopefully soon,' she said cautiously, trying not to commit to anything.

'That'll be nice,' said Reuben as he led Amanda out of the room.

'Don't you worry, Reub,' Christian called out to him, light-heartedly. 'I'll carry the truck!'

*

In the garden, another pretend game of chess ensued under the partial supervision of Walter. Everything in the house had run like clockwork since Amanda's arrival and she wondered how on earth the residents could bear it. For her, such repetition would make her stir crazy. She wondered who it was that possessed the greater problem – the home's elders who were happy to relive the same day over and over, or her for not being able to tolerate such a mundane existence. After all, maybe normality was all these people wanted after experiencing such sadness in their lives.

Amanda sat beside Malcolm on the swing. His movement was

so unnervingly rare that he barely even blinked. Nearby, Christian sat playing a game of top trumps with Reuben, the theme of that particular pack being monsters. Upon looking at his final card, on which a unique illustration of a panther prowled with a menacing snarl, Christian became momentarily distracted by its detail, so much so that he failed to register the words Reuben had spoken.

'K-Kistian,' said Reuben, nudging Christian back into reality.

'I'm sorry. What?' he asked.

'Strength eleven,' said Reuben, as he monitored Christian's response.

Christian looked down at his card again. The panther had fourteen strength points, but he hunched his shoulders forward, feigning dejection.

'You trumped me!' he lied, leading Reuben to raise his fists in triumph.

Amanda clapped and cheered.

'Well played,' said Christian. 'Put them back in the box now,' he instructed, slipping his card within the pack so it could not be detected.

'Can we play again?' asked Reuben, hopefully.

'You can if Amanda doesn't mind. I need to go and get David,' he announced.

To these words, Reuben looked instantly panicked.

'You're letting D-D-David out?' he asked, clearly worried.

Amanda noticed that Reuben was ill at ease.

'Yes, Reuben. He can come and play with all of us,' she offered, in an attempt to calm him down.

'I don't wanna p-play with him!' insisted Reuben, who folded his arms and sat sulking on the grass.

From what Amanda had witnessed, it wasn't like Reuben to act in such a way. Christian approached Amanda and spoke under his breath.

'Don't underestimate the boy, Amanda. I mean it,' he warned. 'David may be young but he's very sick and incredibly dangerous. Now, are you sure you want me to bring him out here?'

Amanda took only a moment to consider the question.

'I don't want to live in a world where people can't change. Do you?' she replied.

Christian fell silent for a moment.

'Well… a promise is a promise. I'll go and get him,' was all he said of the matter.

Christian disappeared back into the house with purpose and Amanda took a moment to absorb the land around her. It had been the only day during her stay that the sky was blue and free from clouds. In the golden glow of sunlight, the setting was truly idyllic. The people in the home were most certainly quirky, but she had grown to love much about them and despite initially finding the place rather creepy, she had finally given in to its charm. Sure, if she were to run a care home it would be fundamentally very different, but she already knew she didn't have the temperament for such a lifestyle and anybody who did deserved to be applauded.

Amanda started up another game of top trumps and as she ran things through in her mind, she knew her work within the home was almost complete. All she had to do was see David – now the only person in the home she had yet to meet – and then she could form a full opinion of the home and get back to living her own life; a new life, with her family in waiting.

It was the final straight and the end was in sight. After all, Margaret had recently warned her how dangerous Ellie was and they soon managed to develop a bond. Therefore, how bad could David really be?

As the front door of the house swung open with force, she was about to find out.

CHAPTER THIRTEEN

The Tip-off
Monday 14ᵗʰ February, 1972

'Get off me, you fucker!' yelled David, at the top of his lungs, the echoes of his voice alerting and disturbing each of the children in the yard as he kicked and screamed, trying his best to hurt Christian. Eventually, one of the blows landed as he struck the homeowner hard on the lip. Suddenly, the air around Christian turned blue and even David fell silent, perhaps realising he had gone too far. Christian put his hand to his lip and pulled it away, revealing the boy had drawn blood. David was stocky but had a youthful face. Amanda guessed he would be around 15 years old, but was powerful for his age and the blow he landed would certainly have hurt. Angered, Christian stepped towards him and grabbed his shoulders firmly.

'What have I told you about your language?' he shouted, as he threw the boy forcefully to the ground.

Gordon covered his ears.

Georgina lowered her head in a vain attempt to block out the commotion.

Walter folded his paper, placing it on his seat as he stood. It was clear he expected to be needed.

Reuben cowered behind Amanda.

'It's okay,' Amanda assured him.

'N-n-no, it's not,' replied the boy, his voice trembling.

David leapt back up to his feet and Christian once again stepped towards him.

'Say sorry, now,' Christian demanded.

David did not. Instead, he spat in Christian's face.

'Fuck you!' he yelled, rebelliously, before turning and running full speed down the hill.

'Get back here!' Christian screamed, but the boy had no intentions of stopping.

David fixed his eyes on Amanda and sprinted towards her, veering around Walter, who unsuccessfully attempted to block

94

him. As he drew closer to Amanda, she walked away from Reuben, observing the look of pure hatred that covered David's face as he shot towards her like a bullet.

'Slow dow—'

David launched himself at Amanda, knocking her to the ground before raining down with his fists.

'No. L-l-leave her alone!' yelled Reuben in helpless defence.

David took no notice and chose instead to focus on the bodily attack of his new enemy, aiming to cause as much damage as he could before Christian and Walter reached them.

'You'll never hurt me,' he yelled. 'I won't let you!'

David hit Amanda harder and harder, his rage forever growing.

'What are you doing?' Amanda yelled, attempting to block his punches with her flailing arms.

Still, he hit her, his great power and speed defying his young body. Amanda managed to take the punishment, but when he landed a solid blow to her stomach, she panicked.

The baby!

In a blind fury, Amanda unleashed one almighty strike across David's face, knocking him backwards onto the ground where he held his head and rolled around, crying in pain. Christian pulled him up by his collar, unsympathetic of his wound.

'Are you all right?' asked Walter as he placed his hand on Amanda's shoulder, struggling to find his own breath.

'I… I couldn't get him off me,' Amanda muttered in mild shock.

She looked to the top of the yard where both Karen and Margaret had emerged to witness the scuffle. Margaret looked every bit as mortified as Amanda felt. Karen, by contrast, stood in utter glee.

'I guess we can forget about those trips into town,' scoffed Karen.

'I couldn't get him off me,' Amanda repeated, as though trying to justify what she had done – to herself above anyone else.

'Leave me alone. Leave me *alone*!' screeched David as Christian dragged him back up the hill.

'You must really like that room, boy!' Christian goaded.

'No!' screamed David, the fear in his voice was there for everyone to hear.

Amanda paced nervously in her bedroom, adrenaline still pulsing through her veins.

'I can't believe I did that. I can't believe I hit a child! I should've restrained him,' she blurted, highly emotional.

'Sometimes it's difficult, my love,' consoled Margaret.

'But you wouldn't have hit him, right?' she retorted, looking towards her ally in hope.

Margaret's silence confirmed as much.

'I can't do this,' insisted Amanda. 'I can't look after these children.'

Margaret shut the door and grabbed her firmly by the arm. It was an uncharacteristic moment that took Amanda fully by surprise.

'I know why you're here,' she said, looking the young woman straight in the eyes.

'Wha… what do you mean?' asked Amanda, on the back foot.

'Come on, love. I've been a carer as long as I can remember and from the minute you arrived, I knew you were different. No. You wanted something else,' said Margaret, knowingly.

Amanda frowned in the way that guilty people did when they had been caught out, partly wondering how she had been rumbled and also trying to muster another lie that would allow her to elude the truth. Margaret looked towards the wardrobe with a raised eyebrow.

Damn it! Thought Amanda, angered by her sloppiness. *I should've been more careful.*

'I checked your room, dear,' Margaret confirmed. 'Sorry for the intrusion, but I was curious.'

'What, uh… what do you want me to say?' asked Amanda, somewhat sheepishly.

'Nothing. I want you to listen,' Margaret informed her. 'I read your journal and you're wrong! You hear me? The children *are* abused here. They suffer every single day,' she admitted, sadly.

'What?' asked Amanda, shocked by the admission.

'If you turn away now, it would all have been for nothing,' she declared.

As Margaret's words sank in, Amanda realised the enormity of her confession.

'I'll send for help,' she said.

'It won't work!' Margaret dismissed. 'They'll cover it up, just like they always do! You've been here for days looking for them to do something wrong and even *you* believed they were innocent.'

'Why are you telling me this?' asked Amanda.

'Because it's gone on for too long,' she said, her words tinged with regret.

Amanda tried to clear her mind.

'Come with me!' Amanda suggested.

'I can't.'

'We can go to the police. You can tell them everything you know!' she encouraged.

'Amanda, I can't! I'm the only one who cares for these kids. I can't leave them, even for a day. And I can't turn against my son,' she said, the pain and difficulty of her position threatening to tear her apart.

'Then tell me everything you know and I'll go and—'

'You don't understand. You hit David, which means he'll think you're one of them now. He won't *let* you go!' Margaret revealed.

He?

'Who?' asked Amanda.

Margaret did not respond.

'Maggie, who won't let me go?' she repeated.

Margaret turned her back and walked towards the door, lingering in the doorway.

'When you know the answer to that,' she said. '…you'll have all the information you need.'

And with that, she left.

Amanda's instincts had been right. It was fate that had led her there and as she recounted all the lies and deceit that had been pushed her way, a surge of anger filtered through her body and a feeling of sheer determination washed through her.

*

Amanda walked around the home as she contemplated what actions to take. Now that Margaret had confided in her, every corner of the house seemed as sinister as it did on her arrival.

She thought of all the details she knew to be true – a lock on each of the children's doors, an isolation room and a host of quirky carers who had withdrawn themselves from society. The lack of visitors had given them free reign to dish out any form of treatment they saw fit and the number of bodies in the graveyard seemed to confirm their torment had often gone too far. Amanda stepped outside and looked at the land around her – hills, fields and dirt tracks for as far as the eye could see, and not a single house or person in sight that wasn't involved in the running of the home. She could scream and shout at the top of her lungs and still nobody would hear her. As an aside, the beast that the locals spoke of could well have been the very same grisly creature she saw through the window. Amanda replayed Margaret's warning. *"You don't understand… He'll think you're one of them now… He won't let you go!"* Was she referring to this animal and, if so, why would it be so concerned with what was happening within the home? These questions made her shudder as a cold chill ran down her spine. She considered the possibility of the beast watching her from the surrounding borders and it caused the hairs to stand up on her arms and on her neck. She looked around, paranoid and semi-manic, suddenly expecting to see a creature from out of this world stalking her.

It was clear now. She was in the middle of an incredibly dangerous situation and leaving may not be as simple as she'd first thought. Even if she could leave, she had no conclusive proof that anything was amiss within the home. Were an officer of the law to ask Margaret about what she'd revealed, there was no guarantee she would repeat it. She'd already said she couldn't turn against her son and in any case, it would be her word against the others. She would be outnumbered by a group of cold, cunning, manipulative people who would surely react vengefully to her betrayal. Amanda couldn't allow Margaret to be threatened. No… she had to find *something* to support her story, and as she scanned the natural prison around her, searching for inspiration, her eyes landed on Malcolm, who had again been left alone on the swing. From a distance, she studied his legs, which powered his slow but steady movement. He was capable of more than he let on. She was sure of it, and so she moved across the yard to test her theory.

'Malcolm?'

He did not flinch.

Amanda looked back across the yard to check that nobody was watching. Walter appeared to be doing a crossword, in which he inexplicably tried to involve Gordon and Georgina, meaning they were all suitably distracted.

'Malcom, I know you're in there. Give me a sign you can hear me,' she said, sounding a little desperate. 'How can I get through to you?' she asked, her exasperation leading her to give up early and step away.

Amanda breathed heavily, her heart pounding as the magnitude of her plight started to take a hold of her. It had been a very long time since she had cried, but through a combination of fear and frustration, she was getting close.

'Who's out there, Malcolm?' she asked, more for her own benefit than his. 'Who's out there?' she repeated. 'Who's Maggie talking about?'

It was at that moment, just as Amanda was becoming overwhelmed with helplessness and pending defeat, that she felt a hand place itself on her shoulder. She froze. No longer could she hear the squeaking of the swing, and as Malcolm leant in, he whispered a name into her ear that she had heard once before.

'Elijah.'

CHAPTER FOURTEEN

Checkmate
Monday 14th February, 1972

Amanda turned to see Malcolm looking down at her. When stood, he was even bigger than she'd realised.

'Who's Elijah, Malcom?'

With his face still free from expression, he turned around and reclaimed his favourite of the two swings.

'Who's Elijah?'

She moved towards him and looked him in the eyes but they had glazed over once more and he resumed the slow, calculated movement that seemed to relax him. Feeling he had said all he was prepared to, Amanda turned and approached Walter with intent.

'Walt, I wondered if you would mind watching Malcolm while I spend a bit of time with these two?' she suggested.

He looked up from his crossword puzzle and shrugged.

'All the same to me,' he admitted, before getting up and making his way towards the other garden.

Amanda sat on the bench next to Georgina, choosing her words carefully.

'Whose go is it?' she asked.

'Georgina's go,' said Gordon, as though he had been waiting to answer the question all day. '275 days. It's a draw.'

'I used to play chess when I was a girl,' Amanda added.

'You *are* a girl!' said Georgina.

Amanda smiled and playfully nudged Georgina with her shoulder.

'When I was a much *younger* girl,' she confirmed. 'Got quite good at it, too.'

Amanda took another glance around the garden, towards the house, in particular. Believing nobody was watching, she put her hand on one of the pawns and picked it up. Georgina firmly grabbed a hold of her wrist.

'Put it back!' demanded Georgina in a threatening bark that took

Amanda by surprise.

'I'm sorry, but nobody was playing so I thought maybe I could have a go,' Amanda explained.

'Uh-oh! She touched the piece,' said Gordon, his expression a combination of confusion and concern. 'Uh-oh!'

'Don't need to move the pieces,' argued Georgina.

'Well, if you don't need to move the pieces, you don't need this one, do you?' Amanda quipped, referring to the pawn.

'Uh-oh!' continued Gordon.

'You seem like a bright girl, Georgina. Why don't you like to talk?' she asked.

''coz I *am* bright,' came her answer.

'You should definitely put it down now,' advised Gordon. 'M-m, h-m. Put it down and walk away.'

'I'll make you a deal,' Amanda teased.

'What?' asked Georgina with interest.

'If you let go of my arm, I'll tell you.'

Georgina took a moment before letting go. Bright white finger marks remained imprinted over a temporary patch of salmon-pink skin. Amanda studied it for a moment before retracting her arm, wisely leaving the pawn on the board.

'I was just talking to Malcolm, and—'

'He wouldn't talk to you!' Georgina interrupted.

'Oh really?' asked Amanda, curiously. 'Why do you say that?'

'Because you're one of *them*,' confirmed the girl.

'One of who?' pressed Amanda.

'You hit David!' accused Georgina.

This perhaps explained why Georgina had become so snippy towards her, but more importantly, the child's words echoed Margaret's recent caution.

'Uh-oh!'

'Do people hit you?' Amanda asked of the children.

Neither of them answered.

'Gord... do people hit you sometimes?' she repeated, targeting the child she believed to be the most likely source of information.

'No. People don't hit me, no. Definitely not,' he replied, his response seeming genuine.

Amanda thought hard.

'Does Malcolm talk to you?' she asked, again aimed at Gordon.

101

'Sometimes... yah!' he answered.

'*Gord!*' Georgina snapped.

'Uh-oh!'

'Does Malcolm ever talk to you about... you know... *him*?' Amanda furthered.

'Who?' asked Georgina.

'You know who,' stated Amanda, confidently.

'I think she knows,' Gordon observed. 'Yah, I definitely do.'

'She doesn't know,' argued Georgina. 'She *can't!*'

'Yah! I definitely think she knows,' he countered. 'Uh-huh!'

'What do you know about him?' Amanda ventured.

Georgina tried her best to act aloof, to which Amanda responded by leaning in and talking under her breath, creating the illusion they were all part of a big secret.

'Elijah,' she revealed.

Georgina was stunned to hear her say the name, forcing her into a thoughtful silence.

'I want to help you, but I need you to talk to me,' Amanda admitted.

'He's always there,' began Georgina. 'Watching...'

'Yah!' agreed Gordon.

'He wants to help, too... but he's scared,' continued Georgina.

'We're all scared,' added Gordon.

'What's Elijah scared of?' asked Amanda.

Georgina's pigmented eyes looked directly into Amanda's with a level of intensity that gave her chills.

'Open your eyes, Amanda!' said Georgina, gruffly. 'He's afraid of *them!*'

'Yah! We're all afraid of them,' supported Gordon.

Suddenly, a loud smashing noise came from the house, as though a thousand shards of glass were dancing on the ground. It was followed by the most harrowing of screams.

Amanda rushed inside and made her way to the first floor landing, where Christian blocked Margaret's path to Reuben and Georgina's bedroom. From next door, Ellie could be heard screaming manically, although her cries were being largely ignored.

'What's going on?' asked Amanda, completely perplexed.

'What are you doing here?' snapped Christian, his eyes studying the empty staircase behind her. 'Where are the children?'

Amanda was drawn to the soft movement coming from the bedroom over Christian's shoulder. She tried to peek around him through the small crack of the door, to which he responded by pulling it shut.

'Is Reuben okay?' asked Amanda, having completely ignored his question.

Christian grabbed her shoulders, tenderly but firmly.

'Listen to me,' he began, gently shaking the distraction from out of her. 'Listen! You *have* to go and protect the children. Now! Bring them into the house and stay together. If they're outside, they're not safe!' he said, gravely.

Finally, she noted the seriousness of the situation.

'What's happening?' she whimpered.

'Just go!' he shouted. 'And you Mum. Go with her. *Now!*'

The combination of intrigue, fear and dread that both Margaret and Amanda felt was overpowered by the urgency with which Christian spoke. They knew that, above anything else, they must act… and fast. Together, they turned and ran down the staircase. Once out of sight, the worry that Christian portrayed on his face disappeared and calmly, he turned around and opened the door to Reuben and Georgina's room. Shattered glass lay on the floor beneath the window. On the walls, the unmistakable claret of blood had splattered in unquantifiable amounts. Walter cradled Karen in his arms, offering strength to the woman who, at that moment, having buckled on her faltering knees, seemed to have none. Beneath Karen, small blotches of blood were drizzled across the floor like a Jackson Pollock painting, slowly soaking into the wood. The blood did not belong to her. Walter rocked with her gently, like a parent trying to comfort an unhappy child, although she did not seem particularly upset. In fact, she didn't really appear to harbour any overwhelming emotions. She was simply vacant. Walter moved his hands to hold his wife's head, drawing her gaze to meet his.

'Tell me it was him,' he said, speaking more in hope than expectation.

'Of course it was,' she said, calmly. 'Who else would it be?'

Walter looked to Christian, the two men exchanging uncertain glances before Christian surveyed the room.

'I'll have Arthur clean this up,' were the words that eventually left his mouth.

*

Downstairs, the nervous energy possessed by Margaret and Amanda had made its way into the children, who they had gathered in the kitchen. All doors and windows had been bolted shut and, collectively, the residents sat on tenterhooks.

'Do you have any idea what happened?' Amanda asked of Margaret, under her breath.

Margaret's unrest was clear and fell so deep that she was unable to speak. She simply shook her head and waited in silence.

'Who's Elijah?' Amanda prodded.

Margaret looked worriedly towards the children.

'We don't have time to be sensitive!' Amanda exerted. 'If you want me to help, I need to know.'

Margaret took a moment to consider the request but just as she seemed ready to speak, Christian entered the room surrounded by an aura of darkness.

'I have some terrible news,' he began.

Amanda's heart skipped a beat. It was as though she were in the midst of an accident that she could see unfolding before her, like a car crash in slow-motion that she was powerless to prevent.

'Reuben died in his sleep,' he said.

The words Christian had uttered were so great in magnitude and so completely lacking in sense that the reality simply didn't register. Amanda's silence was shared by all else in the room. Margaret turned away, her hands covering her mouth as she cried silent tears.

Georgina lowered her head, crestfallen.

Although Malcolm remained physically unaffected, Amanda felt certain she could see sadness in his eyes.

Gordon developed a deep frown as he tried to process the information.

'No more Reuben?' he asked, in a heartbreakingly innocent way.

'No more Reuben,' replied Christian, sensitively.

Finally, as Amanda absorbed the sorrow that surrounded her, something began to happen. She felt tingles creep through her body as though her blood were transforming into small metal pins.

No more Reuben? But how can that be? I sat and played cards with him only hours ago!

Georgina sobbed, prompting Margaret to approach, rubbing her shoulder and caressing her hair in the same way she always did when the girl needed to be comforted, but this time, it didn't work. It wasn't long before Margaret was bent double over the girl, their bodies shuddering in unison as they shared tears over the terrible news. This was no nightmare from which Amanda would awake but a cold, hard reality that had paralysed her in a way she had never known before.

'H-how?' was all Amanda could force from her dry mouth.

'He was having a nap in his room and it appears he swallowed his tongue,' replied Christian, calmly.

'I heard something smash...?' Amanda added.

'Yes. Karen went in to check on him and when she saw his body, she was so upset, she lashed out,' he claimed.

'But, he... it doesn't...'

Amanda's words deserted her. The grief finally kicked in as a mixture of disappointment and sadness blurred her mind and she too began to cry.

'I'll make some calls,' Christian informed them, dutifully. 'We'll hold a service as soon as possible.'

Within the bleakness, Amanda found a moment of clarity. Her face revealed as much as she looked towards the ground floor hallway. Without saying a word, she walked away from everyone. Her actions appeared peculiar to Margaret, who could tell that the young woman was carrying a strange energy.

'Amanda?' asked Margaret, weakly.

She didn't respond. Instead, she took slow, calculated steps towards the corridor, walking past the staircase as she journeyed down the hall. Slowly, but noticeably, her legs gathered momentum. Christian followed her, seeming bewildered as he observed her actions. Margaret stepped out into the hallway, also.

'Where are you going?' asked Georgina, panicked.

'It's alright, my lovely,' Margaret claimed in as reassuring a voice as she could find. 'You stay here.'

'Uh-oh!' added Gordon, making clear his obvious worry.

Amanda approached the front door, unlocking the latch.

'I wouldn't do that,' warned Christian, but to little effect.

Margaret waddled towards Amanda, grabbing her by the arm.

'What are you doing, my love?' she asked, softly and under her breath. 'I told you. You *can't* leave!'

Amanda looked towards Margaret. Her eyes were blank. Her expressions were disjointed. Margaret no longer recognised the person standing before her.

'Let it try and stop me,' she gnarled.

During the many years Margaret had occupied the home, she had seen it discourage many a person's purity, eating away at the goodness of their soul like a virus hell-bent on destruction. Sadly, it appeared Amanda may be no different as she threatened to snap under the strain that consumed her. Amanda's mental state concerned Margaret greatly, so much so that she stepped away due to her own illogical fear that insanity was infectious. Amanda twisted the handle and the door creaked as she pulled it open. She looked outside and puffed out her chest as she took strides towards the car park and then beyond.

She followed the dirt track down the large grass hill, past the tall tree that hung over the pond and towards the heavy gate. As always, the gate was locked and she knew she would not be able to get through, but the purpose of the exercise was not to leave. It was to see if Reuben's death could feasibly be accredited to a swallowed tongue or if, as she suspected, there was something far more sinister at play.

The gate drew closer and, step-by-step a familiar feeling returned. A nearby rustle in the hedges confirmed it. She was being watched, closely, by something that edged ever closer to her. She knew this with utter conviction because she could feel it, but she did not give in to her impertinent mind. Her focus was on the gate and she intended to reach it without breaking her stride – easier said than done when the rolling of a menacing growl found its way to her ears. Amanda's determination was broken and she stopped dead in her tracks. The growl was momentous, like the sound of a heavy rock being forced out of position, paving the way for an explorer to enter the bowels of some sacred tomb that had lain dormant for many generations. It was frightening. It was profound. It was also, somehow, enthralling, to envisage what type of ungodly creature would make such a sound.

Amanda was no longer in control of her movement. So compelled were her senses that she could do nothing other than turn towards the bush where the noise had come from. She could see nothing, but the presence was awesome. Hidden amongst the wildlife and the shrubbery, she sensed that something was wound up like a mighty spring ready to unleash itself towards her. If it did, she would not stand a chance of survival. Something within her gut made that clear. She was too afraid to look away but her heightened senses told her Margaret was willing her back towards the house.

Grrrrr… grew the sound from the point at which her eyes were fixed, but louder; more agitated; ready to pounce. The bush began to move and Amanda closed her eyes, not through fear but in preparation of the unfathomable force with which she was about to be hit.

From the house, a shotgun was cocked and a *bang!* thundered through the air as a bullet flew into the hedges. No longer did Amanda feel the creature was about to leap. Another shot led the target to scupper away, creating a tremor of green movement as it retreated with urgency.

'Come on! Hurry!' yelled Margaret, crying out to her desperately.

Amanda glanced up at the house. Margaret stood bravely at the top of the hill with an outstretched hand and eyes that were wide with worry.

'*Run!*' she screamed.

Although Amanda was desperate to see what had come so close to ripping her to shreds and sending her into the next world, her legs instinctively sprang back to life.

As clearly as Amanda had heard the animal's footsteps retreat, however, she heard them make a daring return as Christian hurriedly reloaded his gun. She glanced back at the grass mound behind which the beast still eluded sight, expecting it to burst through into the garden she occupied at any moment.

Bang!

Bang!

The footsteps once again galloped away, indicating it had escaped the path of gunfire once more. Amanda reached out to feel Margaret's fleshy palm and together they made their way towards the front doorway, where Walter had appeared, standing alert and ready to close the door once they had entered. Finally, Amanda heard the beast leap through the hedges and land on the ground close behind her. She would have certainly looked over her shoulder if Christian, in his hurry, had not dropped the bullets he was trying to funnel into the barrel of his gun. As he scrambled around manically trying to recover, Amanda knew they may not make it back inside. Therefore, her entire focus had to be on reaching that door. She ran as hard as she could, pulling Margaret – who had unwittingly become a hindrance – along with her. Heavy breaths neared as the predator ate up the ground between them. The situation had become so tight that even Christian stopped fishing for the elusive ammunition and joined them in their race to get back to the house. Amanda felt the hot air of something snapping at her ankles. She believed that on the next attempt, the jaws of the alien being were going to rip her Achilles heel from her leg like a warm knife running through butter. At the last possible moment, Amanda closed her eyes, launched herself and Margaret forwards and hoped they had done enough to escape. As they landed on the hard floor of the downstairs hallway, Walter swung the door quickly behind them. Rather than slam shut, it stumbled against the most solid of objects. Christian immediately assisted in the struggle as, together, they pushed with all of their might.

B-m...
Thud...
Scratch...
Scratch...
Click!

Finally, the door was forced to a close. The monster outside continued to claw at it for several moments afterwards before an abrupt silence surrounded them. It was suddenly so calm it was as though there had been no incident at all. Amanda fought hard for breath, as did everybody else involved in the chase. The fact they were all still alive felt like something of a miracle and as the adrenalin kicked in, Amanda realised the story she had been pursuing had just reached a whole new level.

The Exmoor beast was real.

CHAPTER FIFTEEN

Better the Devil You Know
Monday 14th February, 1972

It seemed inhumane to lock the children back in their rooms at a time of such disarray and panic, particularly Georgina, who had been Reuben's roommate for a number of years. Therefore, the elders allowed Gordon and Georgina to play games at the dining room table where Malcolm sat idly beside them. That way, they were together and within sight should the beast make a return. Ellie and David were considered to be safe due to their highly secure proximity within the house and so were, as usual, left to their own devices.

In the living room, the atmosphere was badly strained. Amanda sat in numb silence as Karen pushed for a reaction.

'I told you she couldn't be trusted!' Karen reminded everyone. 'She's reckless and her actions put us all in danger!'

'I didn't... I-I didn't know...' Amanda mumbled, softly, barely able to muster the energy to defend herself.

'I did tell you to keep the children safe,' Christian admitted, sounding sympathetic but disappointed. 'What exactly were you trying to achieve out there?'

'She was irresponsible. As usual!' goaded Karen.

'Go easy on her,' pleaded Margaret, looking hopelessly uneasy.

'We have been,' insisted Karen. 'That's precisely the problem!'

'What was that thing?' asked Amanda, distantly.

The room fell silent.

Amanda shuddered as she relived how close she had come to a certain and grotesquely violent death.

'I don't know what it is,' Christian finally answered. 'But it roams the moors and has done so for many years. It seems to pay special attention to us... and our children.'

'I... can't believe it's actually real,' gasped Amanda, stopping with a sharp breath. 'It's real. It's real...' she said, her voice trailing off as a look of realisation washed over her face. 'And

Reuben?' she asked, her mind piecing things together like a dark, distorted jigsaw puzzle as she processed the wave of information flashing through her mind.

Suddenly, Karen slinked away, her eyes looking any which way but Amanda's direction.

'Yes,' admitted Christian, with a delicate whisper.

'So what was all that nonsense about him swallowing his tongue?' she snapped, angrily. 'Lies!'

'I was trying to spare you the details,' he informed her.

'These are not the kind of details you can choose to omit!' she said, suddenly raising her voice. 'You don't have the right!'

'Don't come here and tell us what we can and cannot do!' argued Karen. 'We have a certain way of living, of working, of doing things so that there can be unity on our land and our methods were chosen for a reason,' she scorned.

'Your methods?' repeated Amanda in pure disgust. 'A young boy was killed because of your incompetence. I could have been killed! And how many others in that graveyard are there because of this... *thing*?' asked Amanda.

Amanda looked to Margaret, whose reaction suggested the beast was responsible for a great many deaths.

'When are you going to do something about it?' asked Amanda, exhausted and close to tears.

'Might I add...' began Walter, as calm and collected as ever. 'That we have told people about this. We've told them repeatedly, but they don't want to listen,' he claimed. 'You sit out there and read the papers with me. You see the scepticism involved at the mention of there being an Exmoor beast.'

For a moment, Amanda wondered if this was what sparked Walter's infatuation with the news. Was he reading updates on the situation as he, like everybody else in the home, had developed an obsession with it? Either way, the scrutiny with which Walter analysed words meant that the few he actually spoke were invariably true. Suddenly, Amanda recalled her own dismissive response towards the radio broadcast that aired on the day of her arrival. Somewhat uncomfortably, she questioned whether anybody would even believe her.

'That's why we take things into our own hands,' revealed Christian.

'Why don't we call the police?' asked Amanda.

'Oh! A wonderful idea!' snorted Karen mockingly in the background.

Christian looked at Amanda with sincerity in his eyes.

'Come with me into my office and call them if you like,' he said, openly. 'Tell them that the beast of the moors has murdered a young spastic child and see what they say.'

'The murder of any child has to be taken seriously!' Amanda returned, incensed.

'If only that were true, dear,' added Margaret, with deep regret. 'But it's like I told you. Nobody cares for these kids except us. Nobody,' she repeated, somewhat ominously.

The confidence of Christian's words and the backing of Margaret, who she fully trusted, was enough to make Amanda believe they had truly taken such measures before, but to no avail. Christian walked over to Amanda and held her shoulders. This time, he did so gently.

'By all means, feel free to try. Maybe their attitudes will have changed,' he said.

Amanda did not expect Christian to be so encouraging about the involvement of the police and his support led her to conclude it would do no good. The local police were either inept, were friends of the family or had genuinely no concern over a group of physically and mentally ill children who did not integrate within their society – especially when the country continued to go through such political turmoil.

Amanda sighed, frustrated and torn.

'Reuben's gone, Amanda, and not a single thing we do can bring him back,' said Christian, tenderly. 'But I promise you this. I'll get two of the best hunters I know here tonight and with them, I will scour the moors until we find the beast. We'll kill it, once and for all. It will end tonight.'

Amanda considered his words. He spoke bravely and although Margaret had revealed there was a level of abuse within the home, Amanda could still only guess who the guilty parties were. Could it be that Christian was, in fact, good? She had seen him play so sweetly with Reuben earlier that morning and was touched by his caring nature. He appeared to be hurting every bid as much as Amanda was and so she wondered if his pursuit of the beast should be encouraged. After all, surely the family were not capable of the same torment as the animal that lingered outside. Once the beast was out the way, she would be able to figure out more clearly how to expose the abusers within the home, and so she looked back to Christian with vengeance in her eyes.

'You need any help?' she asked.

*

As the sun faded on what had been an extraordinary day, Christian sat out the front of the house on a wooden rocking chair. It offered him the perfect vantage point of the land around him and with his trusty gun locked and loaded, he observed, affording the other residents as much peace of mind as he could possibly offer.

Inside the house, Amanda made her way grimly upstairs and towards Ellie's bedroom. The poor girl had, quite rightly, been delirious with fright after Reuben's savage murder and yet such was everybody's panic, no one had thought to console her. Had Ellie's window not have been so high and so small, she might have been able to offer Amanda some vital information regarding the attack. By that same token, had her room been more accessible then it may have been her window through which the beast climbed.

As Amanda passed Reuben and Georgina's bedroom she again heard movement coming from inside and took it upon herself to investigate. She pushed the door gently to see Arthur sweeping remnants of glass from underneath the window. He was also armed with a large bucket of soapy water, which was desperately needed for the large patches of blood that had soaked into the floorboards where Reuben appeared to have fallen. Amanda wondered how much of the poor boy's body the beast devoured and how much of the torment it inflicted on the child would have been for some form of sadistic pleasure. *Why would this happen to such a sweet and innocent boy?* She thought, hoping dearly that his suffering was minimal.

Part of Amanda wished to make her presence known to Arthur

so she could help him with the cleaning, but it was all too painful and so she convinced herself Ellie needed her more and silently edged away.

Once again, Ellie did not attack Amanda as she entered her room. What's more, upon seeing Amanda, she did not turn away. Instead, her bottom lip quivered and she began to cry, allowing Amanda onto the bed where she adopted Margaret's technique of running her hands through the youngster's hair.

'Why?' asked Ellie in between sobs.

'Sshh…' comforted Amanda, soothingly, like the sound of small waves breaking gently in the ocean. 'It'll be okay,' she said, feeling foolish as she did so.

Why did people always say such things at the most inappropriate moments?

'Don't say that!' said Ellie, calling Amanda on her clumsy words. 'It's *not* okay. And it never will be!' she shouted.

The girl gave no warning before pulling away and jumping to her feet. Before Amanda absorbed what was happening, Ellie had run to the edge of the room and was clawing at the padded walls.

'What are you doing?' asked Amanda, with a sense of urgency.

Ellie was frustrated that she could not break through the fabric but started to aggressively head-butt the wall in any case.

'Ellie!' called Amanda, as she ran to the girl's assistance, entering another tussle. The youngster tried desperately to fend Amanda off. She shouted and screamed but Amanda held firm and eventually managed to take her to the ground.

'Ellie, calm down!' she pleaded.

Eventually she did, though the sobbing continued.

'Make it stop,' Ellie cried, weakly. 'Please make it stop!'

Heartbreakingly, Amanda felt certain the girl was referring to her own life. All Amanda could do was hold her and rock with her until the tears dried up. It was while doing this that she noticed an aniseed ball lying on the floor beneath Ellie's bed. Amanda knew that Walter visited the girl. Indeed, he had openly admitted it when she raised concerns over Ellie's lack of contact with the real world. However, something about seeing the sweet lying there appeared incredibly sinister. Amanda shuddered at the implications.

114

'Does Walter come and see you sometimes?' asked Amanda, as innocently as possible.

There was something about Ellie's reaction – the way she said nothing but quickly nestled her face into Amanda's bosom – that suggested she was trying to hide her expression. Only somebody who had themselves been abused could understand the inexplicable shame felt by a fellow victim, as though *they* were dirty; as though *they themselves* had done something wrong. From that moment, there was no doubt in Amanda's mind that, as unlikely as it first seemed, Walter was one of the key offenders.

*

It had become a desperate time; a deadly game of cat-and-mouse where evil was as likely to come from inside the house as it was from the land around it. If Amanda was to survive, she would need to know who her allies were and, even more importantly, her enemies. Roaming the moors was a relentless killing machine and although she had yet to catch Karen doing anything wrong, she felt certain the woman was capable of much cruelty and horror. Amanda felt it in her bones. Added to that list now was Walter – a man who, somewhat disturbingly, had appeared completely trustworthy. What, then, was Amanda to make of her feelings towards Christian? He was another person she always felt she could trust – a good egg who had learnt everything he knew about decency and honesty from his mother, and Amanda's one true ally, Margaret. Was the reason Margaret refused to "go against" her son the fact that he was innocent or simply because she was unable?

Only one thing seemed certain. Amanda had to make a move and she had to make it fast. Her life, and the lives of countless children who had been wronged in the most unspeakable of ways, depended on it.

CHAPTER SIXTEEN

The Point of No Return
Monday 14th February, 1972

A new vehicle occupied the car park at the Prince Care Home. Inside were the two hunter buddies that Christian had promised to summon to the house. In truth, it was one hunter buddy and his sidekick, whom Christian was meeting for the first time.

Andy was a bit of a rogue whose nose was permanently twisted from all the times it had been broken, but he had won far more battles than he'd lost. He pulled out the lighter that was embedded in the dashboard of his truck and lit up a cigarette.

'I don't exaggerate when I tell you how dangerous this is,' Christian warned.

Joe was in his early twenties. He was tall with wavy hair and model good-looks. His inexperience made him nervous and he sat in the back seat looking like a rabbit caught in headlights as Christian eyed him up and down from the front passenger seat.

'You a good hunter?' asked Christian.

Bashfully, Joe shrugged.

'I'm okay,' he replied.

His lack of conviction irked Christian.

'Okay's no good,' he said, bluntly. 'It'll get you killed.'

'Will you relax?' said Andy as he took a deep puff of his cigarette and blew a large cloud of smoke out of the window. 'The boy's good. He's just a little modest, is all.'

'I'm not paying for modest. I'm paying to get the job done,' said Christian, sternly.

'I won the clay pigeon championships in the county last year,' blurted Joe.

Christian looked back at him wearing a deadpan expression that Joe wasn't quite sure how to read.

'You might have read about it,' Joe continued. 'It was in the paper. I mean, I'm not bragging, but… it was a tough group of shooters.'

'There! You see?' encouraged Andy. 'The boy's a natural.'

'Clay pigeon's, huh?' said Christian, looking increasingly agitated. 'Tell me, did the pigeons have claws? Did they have teeth that were as sharp as razorblades? Did they come right at you with the intention of ripping your throat out of your fucking neck?' he asked.

'Jesus!' recoiled Joe, more than a little unsettled.

'You said he was a hunter!' stormed Christian before climbing out of the car.

'Whoa-whoa-whoa-whoa-whoa!' said Andy who, at the prospect of missing out on a payday, suddenly appeared a lot more focused. 'Settle down! The kid's a good shooter. One of the best I've seen. I can absolutely vouch for that,' he assured Christian, who stood at the open door of the truck looking back at them. He monitored the two men closely for several seconds before eventually pulling out a brown envelope.

'Half now. Half when it's over,' said Christian, holding out the envelope.

'I'm good with that!' Andy agreed, eagerly reaching for it. Upon placing his hand on the small package, Christian pulled the man close.

'And who do you tell about this?' he asked.

'No one,' answered Andy.

Christian eyeballed him for added effect before finally letting go of the money.

'Good,' he said with a nod before looking back to Joe. 'Good luck!' he said, somewhat ominously, before closing the door, double tapping the roof of the truck and walking away.

In the living room, Gordon, Georgina and Malcolm sat in front of the television, one of the home's many bizarre traditions given that the trio was made up of an autistic kid, a blind girl and a boy who had "sleeping disease." There was something about having the TV on in the background that was reassuring, though. It was something of a quirky British trait along with drinking cups of tea and complaining about the weather. More importantly, in this instance, it afforded Amanda the freedom to stand in a quiet corner of the room and hold a private conversation with Margaret, who protectively held a small leather-bound book in her hands.

'I've played it through in my mind and something doesn't quite make sense,' admitted Amanda.

'Yes love?'

'If this beast is what's been eating all the animals around here, well that's one thing. I mean, the mark of a wild animal is to kill when it gets hungry so it can survive… but to surround a home and threaten people? To go *into* that home and take a child? That's something else entirely,' summarised Amanda as she expressed her thoughts.

'M-m, h-m,' Margaret murmured, appearing to get upset.

'Think about it,' continued Amanda. 'Why does something kill? Through hunger, fear or passion, right? They're the only reasons. The children it took. Do we know if they were eaten?'

Only at that point did Amanda notice Margaret's deep unrest. Offending people was always a hazard of a person thinking aloud and with Reuben's passing being so recent, it came as no surprise that Margaret was so sensitive.

'I'm sorry,' said Amanda, as she touched Margaret lightly on her arm.

Margaret, as always, forgave her.

'No. It's okay,' she insisted, sniffing gently.

At that moment, Amanda felt bad about delving further, but to make progress she had to distance herself from the subject and press on. It was a technique she had mastered over the years.

'Maggie?'

'H-m?' grunted Margaret, momentarily distracted.

'Were they eaten?' whispered Amanda, wearing an apologetic expression.

'Oh! No. To the best of my knowledge the children have never been… eaten,' answered Margaret, stalling on the final word of the bizarre sentence she had just spoken.

'I didn't think so. Yet I can't see how the beast is threatened by us, either,' admitted Amanda. 'We're locked away in the house, not challenging it for supremacy or for land. That only leaves passion, and I find that very interesting.'

'How do you mean, dear?' asked Margaret, dumbly.

'It's proof of intelligence!' she said, sounding intimidated but also impressed. 'It means there's a thought process behind its actions. It's emotionally driven. I mean, what kind of wild beast could–'

'Stop calling him that!' yelped Margaret, giving in to her own emotions in a rare moment of weakness. 'Please, I can't stand it,' she said weakly.

'I'm sorry,' said Amanda, uncertain of where exactly the source of Margaret's frustration had stemmed from. 'I'm just not sure of what else to call it,' she admitted.

'He has a name,' Margaret revealed.

'A name?'

'Yes,' she confirmed. 'His name is Elijah.'

Amanda looked at her, speaking delicately as she tried to coax out the all-important information Margaret seemed to possess.

'You know, I keep hearing that name, but no one seems to want to tell me who Elijah is,' hinted Amanda in hope.

Margaret took a moment to compose herself, knowing that the next words she uttered would change life as she knew it forever. In providing Amanda with such a key element of the mystery, she knew there would be no return, but considering the life she was leading, that wouldn't be such a bad thing.

'My grandson,' she finally whispered.

'I'm sorry?' asked Amanda, unsure if she'd heard correctly.

Margaret took a deep breath, built her courage still further and spoke again, this time with authority.

'Elijah is my grandson,' she confirmed.

Being an investigatory journalist, Amanda had learnt many facts in her career that she found surprising. By the job's very nature, it led towards truths that the average person would least expect. The element of surprise was what made a great story and so Amanda was always sniffing around the improbable, the unlikely and the downright illogical in the hope of finding new leads that created something truly special for readers throughout the country.

Nothing in her memory compared to this.

Did Margaret really just say that the *beast* of the moors; the *animal* that preyed upon the home and claimed countless children's lives; the *monster* that had come so close to claiming her own life, was her grandson? The magnitude of what this meant could not possibly be absorbed all at once. Instead, Amanda became silent as she contemplated the significance of such a discovery. Suddenly, the context of every conversation she'd held with the residents – every look they'd given her – had shifted. Things started clicking into place and making more sense, but as it did so, the world in which she lived became less like reality and more like a work of fiction.

Slowly, Margaret lifted her hands and offered the leather book that she had held so protectively, handling it as though it were something truly sacred.

'This should answer your questions,' she said.

As Amanda went to take it, she felt the mild resistance of Margaret's grasp until, eventually, she let the book go. Amanda soon discovered it wasn't a book but a photo album.

Unfortunately for Margaret, she had timed her confession poorly, for standing on the other side of the wall on the ground floor hallway, Karen had been pruning wicks and lighting candles. She had heard everything of Margaret's confession.

Karen looked down at her timepiece as it ticked rapidly towards seven.

Darkness.

CHAPTER SEVENTEEN

Hunt or be Hunted

Monday 14th February, 1972

An oil-black sky was illuminated only by the soft bluish glow of the moon that hung rather magically in the air.

Two torches passed over the moorland like lighthouses seeking ships at night as Andy and Joe huffed searchingly through the fields and into the periphery armed with chunky, heavy weapons.

'What'd he say? It was like a panther?' asked Joe, still feeling uneasy about the hunt.

'Something like that,' shrugged Andy, who chewed on a toothpick as he scanned the land.

'And he can't catch it himself?' questioned Joe.

'He's been trying,' Andy informed him. 'Said he came pretty close once, too, but it got away. All he ended up with was the beast's damn claw!'

The search had been going on for forty minutes and Joe wondered how long they would continue before calling it a night. Not wishing to be considered as a whiney hunting partner or a chicken, he refrained from asking such question. Instead, he observed.

Andy was an expert huntsman and his beady eyes gleaned clues that Joe would never have seen. Whatever logic Andy had implemented into the search eventually led them to a rather distinctive footprint that clung firmly to the soil. Andy observed it, put the back of his hand to it, felt the earth with his fingers before sniffing the end of his fingertips. It was a bizarre ritual that, again, Joe didn't dare question. His own personal skills ended at being a good shot and he was fine with that.

'It's fresh,' Andy somehow determined, raising his weapon, readily.

Out of worry, Joe did the same, anxiously looking around with every sense heightened. Suddenly, he noticed endless distractions. Infinite, identical trees made navigation impossible, an owl hooted, birds flapped their wings and insects could be heard calling – none of which Joe had noticed a short moment earlier. Funny how things seemed so different when one became spooked.

The men shone their torches one way, then the next. Finally, they heard significant movement coming from a nearby bush, which shook as they quietly observed it. Andy signalled for Joe to approach from the right as he slowly flanked from the left.

Christian was right. Thought Joe. *This is nothing like clay pigeon shooting!*

An eerie silence ensued as they slowly approached the bush, but Joe's attention was diverted to a flailing branch of an overhanging tree, on which the leaves were wet.

What is that? Wondered Joe as he observed the liquid substance, which glistened as he shone his torch upon it. He edged closer to get a better look and became confused when another stream of the white, gooey substance dripped onto the leaves from above. Joe couldn't help but look up. He saw a dark figure cowering on the branch. His heart told him the being was scared, but his head told him any hesitation could be fatal and so, instinctively, he fired. In retaliation, the beast threw itself on top of Joe, grabbing him firmly and biting into the flesh of his neck before rolling with him on the floor. The beast dictated the movement and ended up on top of Joe, standing on its two back legs and raising a sharp rock in the air before using all of its might to hit Joe repeatedly over the head. The makeshift weapon caused manic screams that soon disappeared, as did the solid structure of Joe's pretty skull, which caved upon the impact of a particularly forceful strike.

It all happened so fast that when Andy finally managed to shine his torch on the being, it prowled towards him, its eyes black with evil and its mouth drooling in bloody excitement as it snarled, paralysing Andy with fear.

This was no panther. It was like nothing he'd ever seen. Not in all his years as a hunter. It was a walking contradiction. Its body was awkward, yet it moved efficiently. It was ugly, yet impressive. It was wild, yet intelligent. It took another step towards Andy as its body swayed like a line of daffodils in a summer breeze, looking almost elegant as it neared its next intended victim. Andy dropped his torch and retreated slowly, managing to keep the same distance between them as he considered his options. Without the light to aid his view, the beast was now an evolving electric blue membrane surrounding a sea of blackness.

Grrrr… it rumbled, backing the man further into the woodland.

Andy had seen how fast the beast could move and it sounded truly riled – a lethal combination for a deadly predator. Andy and the beast were locked in combat and so alert were both hunters that one wrong move would lead to their certain death. Andy knew that if he turned to run, his life would be ended almost immediately. Likewise, his instincts told him that if he raised his gun, the beast would tear him apart before he had chance to pull the trigger. Hunting was about patience; knowing when to attack and when to wait. These were the key skills to becoming a top marksman, and so Andy waited, watching the beast in the same unflappable way it watched him, waiting for a lapse in concentration, a misplaced step, *anything* that would give him leverage and enable him to take the shot.

At the worst possible moment, Joe's body started twitching on the ground. Andy's eyes could not help but flash a quick glance in the corpse's direction. It was all the beast needed to grab a hold of the long barrel and pry the gun powerfully from his enemy's grip.

Cussing his stupidity, Andy was certain he would meet his end. Trembling, he took a deep breath and closed his eyes, wincing as he prepared to be torn apart… but the moment never came. Instead, the beast retreated, slowly stepping back towards the fresh pulsating corpse as it watched Andy disapprovingly. Andy did not know why he'd been spared, but he wasn't about to question such luck and he ran as fast as he could into the night.

*

Certain parts of Exmoor, particularly during the latter hours of night, inspired an incredible sense of isolation, as though it were a small corner of the world that had yet to be discovered; as though man had never existed. It was over such land that Joe's motionless eyes gazed up at the stars as the beast dragged his body behind him. He took it on a very private journey that led to a hidden cave. It was a place the beast knew well.

Once inside, the beast hoisted the body over its shoulder and moped towards a large pit in the ground, into which he lowered Joe's body with great care. Once finished, the beast stood in silence, as if paying its last respects. Its eyes glistened in the dim light and a small stump of a tongue flapped around as it wailed sounds of sadness that echoed through the cave and beyond.

*

Amanda looked toward her window, perplexed. She wasn't quite sure why. Had she heard something? No. Maybe it was just one of those things, like a person who experienced an earth tremor whilst standing outside – the body alerted them that *something* was happening, but with no physical objects such as, say, tables and chairs to dance across the room, there was no visual frame of reference to confirm what the body was experiencing and so the affected party would simply brush their feelings aside and continue with their day.

Amanda was emotionally on edge and was therefore thankful of the privacy she found in her room as she flicked through the photo album Margaret had given her. Each and every picture helped solve a little of the mystery.

There were photos of Malcolm smiling and actively engaging in play with others, snaps of Georgina posing for the camera with beautiful ocean-blue eyes and endless pictures of children Amanda had never met being taken care of by the residents. Finally, Amanda laid her eyes on Margaret's late husband, Stanley – a dashing man with a far-reaching smile.

There were endless photos of Lydia within the album, a woman who seemed to be the main source of everybody's happiness.

Towards the back of the book, however, the inflection of the pictures took a turn for the worse.

There was a shot of Christian sat despondently next to a cot where a small, monstrous hand reached out. Amanda could see that the picture had been taken in the attic. A shaft of light came in at an angle through the window in the roof, shining upon the cot as though its contents were some kind of miracle, but it was not the type of miracle the family embraced.

Amanda turned the page to see further pictorial evidence of the heavily disfigured baby. She had a very strong stomach, but the being – so small and helpless – stirred emotions within her that she did not know how to deal with. All she could do was cover her mouth in horror.

'Oh my God!' she whispered as tears streamed from her eyes.

She grabbed her Dictaphone, thinking aloud at great speed.

'They had a child! Christian and Lydia. His name was Elijah,' she said, her mind feeding her images as it always did when she was on to something. 'There were complications.'

Amanda envisaged the poor deformed baby crying in his cot with Christian stood over him, looking down at the child with sadness and regret. She then imagined Karen doing the same, except her face was bitter, twisted and resentful.

'It's likely Lydia died during childbirth,' Amanda speculated. 'To her loved-ones, it was an injustice that, one-by-one, drove them crazy.'

Amanda paused, closing her eyes as she thought hard. She imagined the attic in which the cot had been placed. She put herself in a reality where Elijah had grown older. She pictured him curled up in the corner of the room, scared and alone.

'Elijah's birth destroyed the family… so they grew to hate him.'

She played out a scenario where the door to the attic burst open and Christian walked in, readying a leather belt to help satisfy his look of retribution. Even her mind's eye wouldn't allow her to process graphic images of Christian beating his defenceless child. The thought was simply too horrid, and so all she could muster were brief, silent flickers of Christian's overbearing shadow against the wall, like an old 8mm film of a man lashing out in silhouette.

'They tortured him,' whispered Amanda, tears of grief creeping from the corners of her eyes once more.

The thoughts that manifested in her head had entered the realm of heavy speculation, but Amanda's one true gift had always been the ability to piece a story together by using seemingly disconnected information. This is what had destined her for journalism.

She pictured Elijah as an adolescent tied to the attic wall in a Christ-like manner. Given that she had not seen the isolation room and had therefore not witnessed the way David had been placed there, the detail she had depicted was uncanny.

In her vision, the abuse and neglect thrust upon Elijah had resulted in his limbs being gangly, his teeth being filthy and his nails long and dirty. She gathered that a person raised in such a state would have minimal body fat and badly malnourished skin. His hair would also be patchy – non-existent in some areas and long and matted through filth in others due to the fact it was rarely cleansed. She imagined the child being ridiculed and degraded by anyone who felt the need to vent their anger. At this thought, somewhat unsurprisingly, an image of Karen popped into her head. She imagined Karen approaching the boy and grabbing his hair firmly in her hand. It would have hurt Elijah greatly but he would have had no energy to fight.

'Look at the state of you, you filthy little beast!' Karen would say.

Beast.

Amanda gathered he got called that a lot. Even those who did not know Elijah and took to writing speculative stories about him in the press used the common phrase "The Beast of the Moors." This would explain why Margaret had reacted so sensitively when Amanda used the term herself. After all, this was the *person* that she lovingly described as her grandson.

'The trauma spread through the family and eventually they started to hurt others,' Amanda continued, with sad confidence.

She was reminded of the plaque on the wall:

THE PRINCE HOME
EST. 1960

'*Most* of them,' she said, quickly correcting herself. 'Not Maggie. She's the only one who cares about these children,' said Amanda, sounding more certain than she felt.

She had believed Christian to be innocent right up until seeing the way he looked over Elijah in the photographs. There was something about his expression – distant yet exuding the sense that a quiet storm was brewing beneath the surface – that made Amanda realise the home could not be run, nor such torture carried out, without him. Therefore, however wronged he might have been in his own life – and some could argue that he himself was a victim – it didn't change the fact he was the glue that held it all together, and for that, he was certainly guilty.

'And maybe Stanley…?' added Amanda.

She remembered the writing on his headstone:

STANLEY PRINCE
A LOYAL HUSBAND AND LOVING FATHER
FOREVER IN OUR HEARTS
1902–1967

"He died of a heart attack, God bless him," Margaret had previously told her.

The happiest Amanda had seen Margaret was when she spoke of her husband, when the love she held for him radiated from every pore of her body. A woman like Margaret would not have remembered him so fondly if he were a bad man, and the fact that Elijah had at some point escaped led Amanda to believe Stanley was partly responsible. She pictured Stanley cautiously entering the isolation room. He would have been doing some good deed such as maybe taking Elijah some food and water. Maybe as he approached Elijah, the boy customarily cowered in the corner, wondering what act of cruelty would be bestowed to him next.

'One day, Elijah had enough…' Amanda informed her Dictaphone, her mind running through endless possible story threads before landing on the one she believed most feasible.

She pictured Elijah studying the wall as a burly shadow grew on its approach. Suddenly, he flexed his claws and launched into his first attack.

'…but he stood up to the wrong person.'

She imagined Elijah turning and plunging his claws into the man's torso, an aggressive surprise that was enough to push Stanley's heart too far. Amanda felt sure that Elijah would have been immediately regretful as he stood by and helplessly watched his grandfather die. He would have looked up and seen the door open and unguarded, maybe for the first time since his birth, providing the perfect opportunity for him to run free. The chances are he would have had no idea what he was running towards. It was very possible he had never seen the world beyond that room, but having nothing to lose he would have taken the chance. He would have roamed the moors as he had nowhere else to go and he would have needed to feast on the wildlife around him to survive.

'And he's lived wild on the moors ever since.'

Amanda remembered Gordon telling her how the "*dog*" would go to his window every night and how he couldn't sleep without him. She recalled Georgina saying how Elijah wanted to help but that he was afraid of "*them*," and how Margaret had said *"he"* wouldn't let Amanda leave because he was likely to have seen her hitting David.

'He's not killing the children,' Amanda concluded with a whisper. 'He's trying to protect them.'

She switched off the Dictaphone and fell into a stunned silence but moments later, the creaking of floorboards outside her bedroom snapped her back into reality.

'Hello?' she called, to which there was no reply.

She looked towards the door, paranoid that something unsavoury was plotting to confront her. It was at that moment she made a decision. When the opportunity arose, she would load the children into Walter's car and get the hell out of there. She suddenly felt that if the children were with her, Elijah would accept she was trying to help them and therefore let her pass. Quite where the children would go, she wasn't sure, but she knew anywhere would be better than there.

Amanda soon considered the alternative – the instance in which she would not be able to get away. The possibility of never leaving the home at all! She knew that if she didn't make it home by the next day then Tony would come for her. That he knew precisely where she had gone and why she was there was the greatest thing she had in her favour. That, at least, offered some consolation.

Quickly, she pulled the textbooks and notebooks from the top shelf of the wardrobe and scribbled one final note to Tony. She skinned one of her pillows of its case and placed the books inside along with the Dictaphone and the photo album. She then examined the floor closely, selecting the loosest of the floorboards to tug at. The wood was quite limber and bent a surprising amount before one of the screws finally broke free of the adjoining wood beneath. Within the hollow flooring, Amanda positioned the makeshift sack into its new secret hiding place and then re-laid the wood back into its original position, making sure it didn't appear to have been moved. She adjusted it a few times, pressing down on it as hard as she could before considering its placement from several angles in the room. Once satisfied that her tampering would not appear obvious, she climbed into bed and attempted to settle.

It would be incredibly difficult to sleep, but she needed to rest, for tomorrow would be the day she finally tried to break herself and the children free.

CHAPTER EIGHTEEN

Buried

Monday 14th February, 1972

Christian had been sat at his desk for only ten minutes morbidly reading a book on coffin designs when the phone rang.

'Hello?' he said, inquisitively, still engrossed in the book as he answered.

'Wh-wh-wh-what was that?' came the panicked voice of Andy, who was fighting for breath. 'What was that?' he repeated.

'I take it you made contact,' said Christian, finally paying full attention to the call. 'I also take it from your tone that you let it get away.'

'You never said it was like that!' claimed Andy.

'You mean you weren't listening!' Christian corrected him. 'I told you it was quick, strong and dangerous.'

'Strong? It's fucking savage!' Andy screamed in anger. 'It took the lad apart,' he added, starting to weep as he relived what had happened.

'Pull yourself together!' snapped Christian, coldly. 'You're supposed to be a professional!

'Fuck you!' Andy cursed, his emotions getting the better of him. 'He's dead. He's dead! And what are you gonna do, eh?'

'You knew the risks,' Christian dismissed, heartlessly.

Andy breathed heavily as he collected his thoughts.

'I want the other half of the money,' he said, boldly.

'You do, huh?'

'Yeah. If not, I'll go to police. And the papers,' he threatened. 'You know I will.'

In order to get Andy to agree to the hunt, Christian had spun an elaborate tale about how he had fallen in love with an endangered animal whilst on holiday. He said he was concerned for the animal – a rare breed of panther – which was due to be put down by its zookeeper and therefore bought it outright and had it transported back to England. Christian claimed that when the local authorities had found out, they demanded he either get the animal put down or send it back to where it came from. Their fear was that the animal would escape into the wild and wreak havoc among the community. Christian said he didn't have the heart to do either and so he let the panther run free. However, due to the number of animals it had recently killed, Christian became concerned that it would cross-breed and breathe life into a hostile new species. This was the only story Christian could think of that tied all of the key points together in a way that was innocently motivated and appeared believable to somebody like Andy, who could never be accused of having the sharpest mind in town. As this yarn was fallacy; a complete work of fiction, Christian was not at all concerned about Andy shooting his mouth off as it would only make him look like a gullible fool. However, the audacity Andy had shown to try and threaten Christian was enough to make his blood run cold, and so he masked the bitter emotions displayed on his face behind the most understanding of voices.

'Forgive me,' started Christian, apologetically. 'I am sorry about your friend. Come back to the house and we'll sort something out,' he agreed.

It took just twenty-seven minutes for Andy to return to the house – something that, if he had any sense, he would never have done. He was down a friend, but up a sizeable sum of money and for a job he had failed to complete. Christian would have let him keep it, too, had he not so greedily tried to push his luck.

As Andy pulled up outside of the gate, Christian saw the envelope of money lying on the dashboard. He told Andy to leave the keys in the truck, saying they wouldn't be long, and then calmly led him up the damp hill.

'Goddamn thing leapt on him from nowhere,' recalled Andy, still visibly shaken. 'And-and-and-and-and it bit down into his neck. I wanted to do something but I-I-I couldn't. I just fucking... froze! You know? I fucking froze, and that's *never* happened before!'

So involved was Andy in his tale that he remained oblivious to the fact he might be in danger, even when Christian led him somewhat conspicuously into the graveyard with his hands hidden in his pockets.

'And those teeth,' continued Andy. 'They looked so sharp and jagged. He had blood...' Andy became emotional once again. 'And the smell...'

As Christian came to a halt, Andy finally looked up and realised where they were. He noticed a large hole dug into the ground at the end of a line of gravestones. His head whipped around, nervously.

'What the hell is this?' he asked, suddenly panicked.

'You know, there's not a single body in this yard that damn beast isn't responsible for, including the young boy we have to bury tomorrow,' said Christian.

'You're burying someone tomorrow?' asked Andy, before breaking into a relieved chuckle and exhaling deeply. 'Man! For a minute there, I thought—'

Christian's movement was so swift and surprising that Andy didn't feel the six-inch blade that was thrust into his stomach – initially, at least – but as the gravity of the situation dawned upon him, the pain became far greater than any broken nose he'd ever suffered.

'I'm sorry to have got you involved,' said Christian, softly, into Andy's ear. 'If there is a God, may he have mercy on your soul.'

Those were the last words Andy would hear as Christian pushed him backwards into the pit. Andy attempted to get up, but a sharp throbbing pain shot from his stomach and prevented him from doing so. As he looked disbelievingly down at his torso, large volumes of blood pumped out of his body. All he could do was apply pressure to the hole in his gut, but the wound was too severe and the blood continued to gush. Christian picked up a nearby shovel and started tossing soil on top of him. Andy screamed, which prompted Christian to lobby the earth towards his head and, with the limited movement Andy was capable of, he was unable to prevent large clumps of the moist mud landing in his mouth. Coughing, spluttering, bleeding, crying and bellowing silent screams, Andy knew it was the end.

Why did I come back here? Was the last thought that crossed his mind.

And then he thought no more.

CHAPTER NINETEEN

Goodbye, Dear Friend

Tuesday 15ᵗʰ February, 1972

Above the earth where Andy's body secretly lay was a small coffin, inside which the remains of the sweet young Reuben had found its final resting place.

A vicar, who was an age old friend of Christian's, gave a sermon as the residents grieved, with the exception of David and Ellie, who were still locked away in their rooms. Amanda would have disputed their absence had the day not been chosen for her getaway. As it was, the less attention she drew to herself, the better. Besides, that moment was about mourning the loss of one of the purest, most endearing little fellows Amanda ever had the pleasure to meet and she believed nothing should distract her from doing so.

Amanda absorbed the size of the coffin as Margaret, who stood by her side, wept uncontrollably. Amanda thought in great detail about what a tragedy it was to bury the young. Her child hadn't even been born yet, but the thought of having to bury her offspring in her own lifetime was something she did not wish to entertain and so she fought her musings away.

The service soon passed and when it reached its end, Christian walked immediately towards the vicar and shook his hand, talking in the soft way people always did at funerals as he thanked the man for his words.

Walter and Karen dutifully ushered the children back towards the house. Karen wore a black veil that hid her emotions, that is if she portrayed any at all. As Amanda watched her, she wondered if Karen had ever shed a genuine tear.

'Are you alright, love?' asked Margaret, selflessly.

'Would you believe me if I said yes?' replied Amanda, somewhat curtly.

Margaret entered an awkward silence.

'I'm sorry,' Amanda quickly added. 'It's just... it's been a crazy few days, huh?' she said, knowing that Margaret would understand her heightened sensitivity.

'You can say that again,' she acknowledged, rubbing Amanda's back as though she were one of the children.

Amanda looked towards the other residents as they exited the graveyard through the flowery archway.

'I need the keys to the isolation room, Walter's car and the gate at the bottom of the hill,' stated Amanda under her breath and in determined fashion. 'I need them within the next hour. Can you help me?' she asked.

Amanda's instant change of tone took Margaret by surprise, but she responded to the urgency by processing the requests as quickly as possible.

'Christian keeps a spare key to the isolation room somewhere in his office, usually in his desk. I'm sure I can find that,' said Margaret, thinking aloud. 'As for the other things, they're a bit more tricky. What are you planning, exactly?'

'I'm going to persuade Christian to go hunting and when he's gone, I'll round up the kids and drive away,' Amanda informed her.

'You're gonna take the children?' asked Margaret, as though surprised.

'Yes.'

Margaret looked deeply saddened by the thought.

'Maggie, when I get word out about what this place is, *everything* will change. You do understand that, don't you?'

Margaret absorbed the words, swallowed hard and eventually nodded her head.

'I guess I just never really thought about it. You know... what comes next,' she admitted, her face falling into a broken smile.

'You want the children to be safe, don't you?' asked Amanda.

'Of course!' Margaret assured her. 'More than anything.'

'Well, if I can get them away from here, I believe they will be,' encouraged Amanda. 'It *has* to be Walter's car for this to work, you understand?' she said, to which Margaret nodded certainly.

'Yes dear.'

'Maggie, if anything should happen to me, I've left a few things in my room. They're under a loose floorboard—'

Margaret shook her head, vehemently.

134

'No. Nothing can happen to you,' she said, as though she were wishing the very thought away.

'Maggie. Listen to me. You have to focus, you understand?' said Amanda, with strong intensity. '*If* anything should happen to me then you *have* to make sure you get my things to someone who will listen. I've written the name and address of somebody in London who will do the rest. His name is Tony King and he's the head of my paper. Just get my stuff to him,' she said, as she looked deep into Margaret's eyes.

'I'm not as strong as you,' said Margaret.

The woman's state of mind did not fill Amanda with confidence.

'Maggie, you're the strongest person I know,' Amanda assured her.

'I can't go against my son,' she said, tearfully. 'I can't do it.'

'This is bigger than us, Maggie! Think of the poor children. They've done nothing wrong,' Amanda reminded her, knowing that if there was a way to make Margaret see more clearly, it was by making her think of the lives that had been ruined. 'Now promise me, *promise me* that if things go bad, you'll do what I asked.'

Amanda knew that she could trust Margaret, if only she would give her word. She nodded her head weakly, but that wasn't good enough for Amanda.

'You have to promise,' Amanda demanded of her.

'I promise,' Margaret finally uttered.

They looked at each other, both women knowing the journey was nearly over. The moment for change was fast approaching and they couldn't do it without one another's help. There was so much love and respect between them, but sadly, circumstances were destined to take them apart.

'Good,' Amanda proclaimed. 'Go back to the house, Maggie. Try to get a hold of those keys. I'll be there soon.'

Margaret nodded, taking a moment to gather her thoughts. She appeared to have the weight of the world on her shoulders. There was so much she wanted to say, but instead, she remained silent and waddled towards the archway with purpose.

Amanda turned her attention back to the grave. She didn't flinch as Arthur entered the yard. In fact, she had anticipated it.

'D-d-do you need more t-t-time?' asked Arthur, who had a

shovel in his hand ready to return the earth to where it belonged.

'No,' she replied. 'Go ahead.'

Arthur stepped towards the grave and started scooping the dirt back into the ground, oblivious to the fact that Amanda was studying him. She noticed the initials *AA* sewn onto the breast pocket of his overalls.

'Do you know Elijah?' she asked, brazenly.

The question made Arthur incredibly twitchy.

'Don't look at me,' she instructed. 'Someone could be watching. Just carry on what you're doing.'

He did precisely that.

'You see, I don't know your story but the fact you live here must mean you know a lot about what goes on,' she figured. 'I want to help Elijah, and judging by the way the family treats you – keeping you at such a distance – I'm betting you're not the greatest fan of how they do things.'

'H-how do you know that n-n-name?' asked Arthur.

'The children told me,' she informed him. 'As did Margaret.'

Amanda studied the coffin with interest. By this time, it had almost been completely covered in soil. Another life washed away, erased from the world with only a headstone to show for it.

'I bet you've seen inside all these coffins, haven't you?' she quizzed.

Arthur stumbled, his downtrodden expression revealing that Amanda's statement was true but that he wished it wasn't.

'How did Reuben die?' she asked.

Predictably, Arthur hesitated.

'Don't wanna t-tawk about it,' he said.

'Neither do I, Arthur, but the family are saying he was killed by Elijah. Are you happy with that?' she posed.

Arthur frowned and shook his head.

'Do you know who killed him?' she pressed.

He took a moment before nodding his head.

'Was it Karen?' Amanda offered, to which he nodded again.

'Is there any proof?' she asked, desperate to know she would be able to make Karen pay for all the evil she had done.

Arthur thought for a moment before shaking his head, much to their mutual disappointment.

'They're good at h-hiding it,' he admitted.

Arthur had become a much more useful source of information than Amanda had anticipated, so she tried hard to think of anything else he might be able to help with.

'And Lydia died giving birth to Elijah, right?'

To this came the most surprising answer of all.

'My sister's not d-d-dead!' he replied, scoffing at her foolish remark.

'Your sister?' she questioned, faintly.

She looked back at the initials on his overalls. *AA*. She recalled Margaret's passion for knitting.

'Arthur Ambrose!' Amanda whispered.

Arthur smiled, mischievously.

'They don't know yet, but she's gonna get out. She'll be b-back any day now,' he said, wearing an excited grin.

'Who? Lydia?' asked Amanda, who could scarcely believe what she was hearing.

Arthur nodded, happily.

'Back from where?' she pushed.

'DCLA,' he enlightened her.

Amanda had heard of DCLA. When she was plotting her undercover assignment, the place had come up during her research of the area.

Devon County Lunatic Asylum.

*

As Amanda learnt of the earth-shattering news, Christian had taken yet another call in his office. The person on the other end remained silent, which had been a frequent occurrence for a number of weeks.

'Is it you?' he asked, partly curious and partly hopeful. 'Is it you?'

He closed his eyes and imagined his wife's lips. She loved to wear cherry lipstick. It was a colour that so suited her. That is what he imagined brushing against the mouthpiece on the other end of the line.

After a short silence, the caller responded.

'Everybody's gonna see what you did,' said a woman's voice, somewhat casually.

Christian sat bolt-upright in his chair.

'Lydia?'

'They will, you know. They're gonna get to see,' she teased, like an adult describing something mystical to a young child. 'They're gonna see what you did,' she said again, before giggling.

'Lydia, wha—'

'Everybody's gonna see what you did!' she shouted, again and then again, screeching rather manically down the phone, reaching such a volume that Christian had to pull the handset away from his ear.

Her laugh was haunting, and in a blurry state of mind Christian placed his free hand on the receiver, causing the line to go dead. The sound of her voice was enough to utterly take the wind from him. Where there was once so much love there was now crippling guilt and endless broken memories that reminded him of what could have been. When Christian lived in the fictitious world he had created – the place where Lydia never existed – he could fool himself into thinking he was okay, but after hearing her voice, he was no longer afforded the luxury of such ignorance.

She most emphatically *did* exist.

Deflated, Christian hunched over in his chair, everything he hated about himself and his God-forsaken life had reared its ugly head once again, and it wanted vengeance.

CHAPTER TWENTY

Closing In

Tuesday 15th February, 1972

Margaret rifled through her keys, removing the one she owned to Christian's office and placing it on a spare key ring she had dug out from the back of a kitchen drawer. *Welcome to Exmoor* said a bold italic font over a picturesque piece of land that sloped down towards the water mouth on a clear summer's day. The picture represented the place Margaret had fallen in love with, but that place had become just a distant memory.

She exited the house from the kitchen and walked around to the side garden, watching secretly through the shrubbery as, at the bottom of the hill, Walter let the Vicar out through the gate. She watched as he placed his keys securely back into his jacket pocket. If she could only get her hands on them for a matter of seconds she could remove the two she needed and return the others to his jacket. By the time he would realise they were gone, the same would be true of Amanda.

So wrapped up was Margaret in wondering how to obtain his jacket that she failed to notice Karen stepping out onto the lawn behind her, looking deeply committed to a focus of her own.

'Oh!' yelped Margaret as she turned around, startled to discover she was not alone. 'I didn't see you there,' she chuckled, nervously.

Karen stood like a stone statue, watching, pondering. It wasn't until Margaret looked down that she saw a short length of washing-line wire coiled in her hand. Margaret shifted anxiously on her feet as her helplessness slowly consumed her. Like a farm animal sensing the arrival of a weapon intended for its demise, Margaret's entire body slumped in defeat, sensing there was no escape.

'Don't you ever get tired of all this?' she asked of Karen, in a self-loathing voice. 'Don't you ever feel guilty?'

Karen considered the question for only a moment.

'Never,' she said, proudly, like a patriotic soldier who'd been brainwashed into thinking their way was the only way.

'And knowing that even if we only did good for the rest of our lives, we would always be judged for what we've done in the past,' Margaret furthered. 'That doesn't make you worry?'

'I take it you're referring to your God?' Karen sneered. 'The one who abandoned us in our time of need? The one who left us to rot?'

'He never abandoned us,' Margaret retorted, softly but defiantly. 'We abandoned him, and for that, we shall never be forgiven.'

'Well, when you see the great Lord,' Karen mocked as she took large, menacing steps towards Margaret. 'Tell him I'm incredibly sorry.'

There was an awkward moment of tension before Karen wrapped the wire around Margaret's neck with incredible speed. She flailed her short, tubby arms towards Karen, who eluded her reach with ease as she spun around, appearing behind Margaret and then pulling hard on the wire as she forced the helpless woman to the ground. Margaret coughed and spluttered, trying desperately to hook her fingers beneath the wire that choked her, but it was all in vain. She soon became dizzy as an excessive amount of blood rushed to her head. It wasn't long before her breaths became weaker and weaker still, until they disappeared forever.

*

With Amanda's latest findings, she ran through the halls of the house with secret urgency.

'Maggie?' she whispered, harshly. There was no sign of her anywhere. She crept eagerly towards the kitchen. 'Maggie?' she called again.

Her search was disrupted by an emphatic shrill that rang through the house; a near identical scream to that which plagued the building moments after Reuben's death. It was a sound that made Amanda's hairs stand to attention. She stepped back out into the ground floor hallway, where the horrid noise had come from. Christian, too, emerged from his office in panic and together they saw Karen lingering in the front doorway, looking distraught.

'What's going on?' asked Christian, taking hold of Karen's arms through fear she would topple over.

'Quite,' inserted Walter, who appeared at the top of the staircase with Gordon and Georgina in tow.

For added effect, Karen stumbled forwards, prompting Christian to support her.

'It's your mother,' groaned Karen as she struggled for breath. 'It's your mother,' she repeated, looking up to him. 'Christian. I'm so sorry!'

Karen placed her arms around his neck as she pulled herself towards him, her body shuddering as she bawled.

'Wha—' said Christian, numbly. 'What about her? Where is she?'

Karen did not reply and so he shook her desperately.

'What happened?' he yelled.

'She's dead, Christian.'

Reuben's passing had come as a complete shock, but news of Margaret's death was the cause of instant grief, the like of which Amanda had never experienced before. Tears rivered down her cheeks as she stood rooted to the spot, observing Karen's elaborate act in horror.

'Wha…? How…?' mumbled Christian is disbelief.

'*She* did it!' accused Karen, as she looked down the hallway, pointing directly at Amanda.

'What?' stammered Amanda.

'Uh-oh!' said Gordon.

'Amanda killed your mother,' Karen declared, with utter conviction.

'No she didn't. She wouldn't do that!' Georgina protested.

'I saw Amanda attack her! Out in the garden, but I was too far away to—'

This time, Karen did dramatically collapse to the ground, forcing loud crocodile tears as both Walter and Christian closed in on the accused.

'No! She's lying!' said Amanda, petrified, as she retreated slowly. 'Can't you see? It's what she does. It's what she *always*

141

does! The same as when she lied about Reuben!'

'The beast killed Reuben!' Christian shouted.

'The beast? Christian. That's your son,' Amanda reminded him, softly. 'Elijah's your son.'

'Who told you that?' snapped Walter.

'You were supposed to be gone by now!' Christian yelled.

The comment confused Amanda.

'What?' she asked, attempting to decipher his meaning.

'Hello? Hello?' said Christian, feigning desperation in an exaggerated voice that made him seem psychotic. 'I… I saw something. Something horrible,' he continued. 'And I don't know what to do. I don't know what to do!'

'You?' Amanda whispered, in disbelief.

The realisation that Christian was the one who placed the call to the editor's office suggested that he *wanted* a journalist in the house.

Of course! Amanda cursed, suddenly realising they had placed an advertisement for a carer knowing she would find it when she followed the lead. *What was I thinking?!*

'Why?' asked Amanda, of Christian's wicked plan.

'You mean you can't work it out? There's actually a riddle Miss high-and-mighty can't solve?' vented Christian. 'Do you have any idea how frustrating it's been watching you swan around here like you had one over on us when, all the while, you followed every trail we laid out for you?'

Throughout the entirety of Amanda's visit she had agonised over how responsible Christian had been for the bad things that happened around him. She had considered whether Karen might be the true driving force of any wrongdoing and wondered if the woman had somehow created a mystical hold over Christian that made him blind to her actions, but suddenly, everything became clear. Amanda had never seen – nor could she have envisaged – Christian being like this. Right before her eyes he had snapped. He had become delirious. His eyes were enraged and black. His outer shell suddenly represented the insides of a secret mad man… and it was absolutely terrifying.

The sight of Karen rising to her feet behind him, wearing a demonic grin, made Amanda acutely aware of her situation. At least two crazed, dangerous killers had rounded on her in the middle of their isolated lair and had unanimously decided that she would become their next victim.

'Christian...' Amanda sobbed.

'No!' he screamed. 'It's my turn to talk now!'

Christian looked towards Walter on the staircase before nodding at the children.

'Lock them in their rooms,' he requested. 'I don't want them to see this.'

'Indeed,' agreed Walter.

As Walter turned to place his hands on Gordon and Georgina, they screamed in full support of Amanda, but it was useless. There was nothing they could do. It did, however, mean that Amanda had one less person to deal with and in her current predicament, any positive news was welcome.

Christian's attention fell back to Amanda, whose backward steps took her into the kitchen.

'You were supposed to go back and write about the beast so people would want to find it and kill it!' Christian revealed.

Despite the bleakness of her own reality, Amanda couldn't help but feel sadness for Elijah. *How could his own father have grown to hate him like this?*

'But... why?' Amanda was compelled to ask.

'Because he ruined *everything*!' yelled Christian with radiating waves of contempt.

'What exactly did Elijah ruin, Christian?' asked Amanda, stubbornly.

'Don't call it that,' Christian demanded, the name chipping away at him and threatening to disrupt the villainous image he had created for his son.

Sensing this, Amanda honed in.

'*It* has a name, and his name is Elijah.'

'Stop talking,' said an agitated Christian.

'And Lydia is still alive, so what exactly has been ruined?' Amanda pressed.

Christian and Karen glanced at one another, taken aback by the extent of Amanda's knowledge.

'Anything that's been ruined has been ruined by you,' Amanda told him. 'Elijah's not the beast,' she continued. 'You are.'

As the bitter words were being exchanged in the kitchen, they were all oblivious to Elijah approaching Margaret's lifeless body in the yard. He stared into her empty eyes as she lay sprawled out on the lawn. He nudged her, but to no avail. Emotionally, he cradled her and shed tears for one of the only people that had ever shown him love. He looked towards the house. Every crevice of the home brought him an unhappy memory. On the nearby ground was a cracked paving slab where Karen had once thrown a heavy duty plant pot at him. As he looked up he saw a wooden board in place of Reuben and Georgina's bedroom window; the window he had smashed in a desperate attempt to stop Karen inflicting the physical cruelty that led to the young boy's death.

Ever since Elijah's escape, he had feared the home in which he was once held captive. Over the years, he had made countless attempts to re-enter the building so that he may put an end to the cruelty once and for all, but so crippling was the fear towards his birthplace it made him physically weak and nauseous as he approached. Thus far, the courage needed to take those final steps and re-enter the home had always eluded him, but if ever he had the motivation to finally conquer his fears and overcome that barrier, it was surely the beloved grandmother lying dead in his arms; the person to whom he owed the greatest debt.

Elijah placed Margaret's limp corpse back down onto the ground, closed her eyes so she was at peace and swaggered to where he could hear a commotion. Through the kitchen window, he saw Amanda edge backwards, cornered by Karen and Christian. It was time to make a stand once and for all, so Elijah walked stealthily towards the kitchen doorway.

CHAPTER TWENTY ONE

The Beginning of the End
Tuesday 15th February, 1972

'You're sick!' declared Amanda, to both Karen and Christian, who wore wrongful looks of excitement as they imagined the type of evil that should never be acted upon. 'You're so disturbed and detached from reality you can't even see how fucked up all of this is!'

'When people find your body torn to shreds, that is when they'll join us,' said Christian, with chilling calm, far too absorbed in his own fantasy to register what Amanda had said. 'Nobody cares when a bunch of retarded kids get murdered. In most cases, that doesn't even make the news, but when a big time city journalist gets killed? Well... they won't be able to ignore that,' he said, proudly, suddenly viewing Amanda in the way a painter might look over his latest masterpiece.

'I can see the headlines now,' he continued, his eyes dancing with excitement. 'There'll be an outcry. *Find the Exmoor beast! Kill the beast! Hunt it down and show it no mercy!* He might be able to elude me, but let him try and hide from a whole country baying for its blood.'

'He didn't kill these children,' protested Amanda. 'She did!'

Karen smiled a superior smile that agitated Amanda.

'Are you really just going to stand by and watch people get murdered, raped and tortured?' Amanda asked of him. 'It's not their fault. And your poor mother...'

'I've heard enough,' interrupted Karen. 'Are you going to put an end to this or shall I?' she asked, forcefully.

'She was so lovely, Christian,' complimented Amanda, in a last-ditch attempt to speak sense into him. 'She was always so nice to me, and whenever she spoke about you or your dad, she would glow.'

Sensing that Christian had started to think too deeply, Karen pulled a large knife from a nearby work surface. Amanda became tense at once, picking up the only thing that resembled a weapon near her – a marble rolling pin. This certainly put her at a disadvantage but at least she had *something*. Karen chuckled at the sight of the poor, innocent lamb. Violence was not something that Amanda embraced and it showed, but what she did have was intelligence and while Karen openly mocked her, Amanda figured it would be easier to survive if her attacker wasn't thinking straight. With that in mind, she aimed to get Karen flustered.

'I warn you,' Amanda goaded. 'Killing me won't be as easy as killing a child.'

'I suspect it will,' dismissed Karen, but as she stepped forwards in preparation of inflicting a fatal lunge, the door that led to the yard crept open and Elijah's familiar growl stole all of their attention.

Karen's face grew demonic as she saw him prowl into the doorway.

'Get the gun!' she barked at Christian, who immediately disappeared down the hallway.

Amanda looked at Elijah with wide eyes. His presence was undeniable, his wildness intimidating and to see him up close was utterly daunting. That the boy was still alive – effectively functioning and somehow immensely powerful – was the stuff of legend. Amanda feared for her own safety as Elijah neared her, stepping into the kitchen, his rage exceeding his fear. She knew that he could tear her apart as simply as she could rip through paper, but thankfully, his eyes remained fixed on Karen and in one frighteningly quick movement he leapt towards her, his force knocking her to the ground. He started by sinking his teeth into her arm, leading her to drop the knife and thus leaving her unable to defend herself. Elijah proceeded to maul her with the might of a lion, unleashing all the years of hurt he had suffered at her malevolent hands.

Amanda seized the chance to run into the hall and up the stairs to the first floor landing as she fumbled through her keys.

'What's going on?' asked Walter, sharply, as he appeared from Gordon's bedroom.

'Uh-oh!' sounded Gordon in the background.

'You're becoming a widow,' replied Amanda, taking great satisfaction in watching his face crumble.

'No...' he whimpered before running down the stairs, calling his wife's name.

*

The old man ran and ran, instantly traumatised by the scene that greeted him. The kitchen floor looked like that of a slaughterhouse, and in the middle of the claret lake, his darling wife's legs shook as Elijah feasted on her flesh.

'You get off her, you demon!' said Walter with the utmost contempt.

Elijah stopped and turned to face him.

They were not the best words he could have chosen and the hatred that filled the old man's veins was returned tenfold.

*

At great speed, Amanda collected Ellie, Gordon and Georgina from their rooms. They were completely in tune with the standoff that took place downstairs and therefore showed how co-operative they could be as they faultlessly followed Amanda's instructions. She led the children to the top of the stairs, from where Walter could be heard screaming in agony.

'Don't listen,' she told the children, before asking them to stay exactly where they were as she made her way up the narrow staircase towards the door to the isolation room. She hadn't managed to attain a key and so she rammed her body against it as hard as she could.

Thunk!
Thunk!
Thunk!

The door was robust and heavy, meaning progress was slow. The children, however, showed initiative and followed Amanda to the top of the steps, helping her bang, kick, push and barge at the door until eventually they broke through. The room was dark and bare and smelt absolutely rotten. At the far end, the outline of David's body could be seen just beyond the solitary ray of light that shone through the window.

'David!' gasped Amanda, shocked to finally see the conditions in which he had been kept.

*

Christian flew out of his office as he cocked his gun. There would be no fumbling for bullets this time, and no more missed opportunities. He made his way to the kitchen with urgency to see the beast atop Walter. So occupied was Elijah in dishing out pain that he remained oblivious to Christian, who slowly raised his gun and locked the beast in his sights.

For Christian, it was a truly noteworthy moment. For so many years he had hunted the beast. For so much destruction was this monster responsible. And it was all about to end.

Christian took a deep breath, allowing him to steady his aim. It was a breath that Elijah heard, leading him to push himself away from Walter as he sprinted towards the back door.

Bang!

Bang!

Begrudgingly, the first shot hit the wooden door of a cupboard, but the second bullet landed and the beast yelped, staggered and fell into the door before forcing its way outside.

Christian reloaded his gun and followed.

*

In the attic, the sound of gunfire had brought everybody to a halt as they listened to what was happening downstairs. They heard a door smack against a wall and then Christian yelling "*Come back here!*" which was enough to let them know they still had time.

Ellie, Gordon and Georgina lingered in the doorway as Amanda anxiously made her way across the attic. She couldn't help but notice the countless drops of dry blood that had settled on the old dusty floorboards, revealing years of untold cruelty. Her mouth dropped open in horror when she saw scores of grisly, primitive

148

tools and weapons hanging from the walls all around the room. It was a torture chamber. There was no other way to describe it, and it made her sick to the stomach. She felt overwhelming guilt for not having forced her way in sooner, but she could ill afford to think about that now.

'David, listen to me,' Amanda instructed, calmly, still a little weary from their previous encounter. 'I'm here to help you.'

'I know,' he sniffled, clearly petrified. 'Arthur told me.'

The knowledge that both Margaret and Arthur had been looking out for the poor boy came as some consolation.

'Is there a light in here?' Amanda asked.

'Yeah,' David confirmed. 'Up on the wall. Near the door.'

'I know where it is,' said Georgina, who didn't need her sight to be able to find it – a clear sign that she, too, had spent some time in the isolation room before the use of her eyes was stolen from her.

Upon closer inspection, Amanda saw that David's chains had a heavy duty lock on them. Without the key, the only other alternatives would be to pick the lock, which she had no idea how to do, or to remove the chains from the wall, to which they were heavily screwed.

'I need something to get these off,' Amanda told the children. 'I need something to break him free!'

Together, they looked through the endlessly horrendous devices. Saws, drills, chisels, files, nun-chucks, bats, knives, pliers – most of which had been tinged with blood. Somewhat sadistically, there was even an operating table pushed against the wall, ready to be wheeled out whenever it was needed.

'What about this?' asked Ellie as she lifted up a large pair of wire cutters.

It wasn't ideal, but it was the best they could find and eventually Amanda managed to use it to cut through the lock. She promptly wrapped David's arm around her neck and led the children back to the ground floor. From the foot of the staircase, Amanda saw the masses of blood on the kitchen floor and quickly shielded the children's eyes. Upon noticing Walter hunched helplessly on the floor fighting for breath, she sensed an opportunity.

'I'm going into the kitchen for a very short while. Stay right here until I come back,' she instructed them, remaining as calm and composed as she possibly could.

Walter was propped awkwardly against a kitchen cupboard taking short, sharp breaths as he covered a nasty chest wound with his hand. His eyes rose to Amanda but he couldn't speak. He couldn't even muster the energy to look angry. He was a defeated man – pale and drowsy – who had been forced to look at his motionless wife's body. There was something almost poetic about it, as though it were his punishment for allowing his wife to lead him towards such sin. For Walter, it was nearly over as he started to slip out of consciousness. Amanda approached him and lowered herself, watching him closely as she checked his pockets. He raised a feeble hand to stop her but was far too weak to be a hindrance. Amanda felt a rush of relief as she located his keys and pulled them out from his jacket pocket. She looked upon the dying man one last time, stood over him victoriously and then finally walked away.

*

Bang!
  Bang!
  'I'm gonna get you this time!' screamed Christian from outside, suggesting Elijah was still roaming free, but Amanda knew they had to hurry.

*

With the children nervously checking the ground floor hallway, Amanda unlocked the door to Malcom's room to see him sat on the edge of his bed in his usual pose: straight back, neck cocked slightly to one side with absolutely no signs of movement, Amanda ran to the foot of his bed, grabbed a hold of his wheelchair and pushed it in front of him.
  'Malcolm, come on,' Amanda encouraged. 'You have to get up.'
  This time, Malcolm did respond but with a simple shake of the head.

'No? What do you mean no?' she asked, pressingly.

'Can't leave him,' he said.

'Who?' Amanda questioned. 'Elijah?'

To this, he nodded.

Amanda thought as fast as she could.

'I'll come back to get him. I promise! But we have to go. Now!'

'You'll come back to get Elijah?' asked Georgina, in excitement.

'Yes!' agreed Amanda, knowing deep down that it wouldn't be a feasible task.

It did, however, provide the children with the lift they needed at the most critical of times, prompting Ellie to approach Malcolm and hold out her hand.

'Come on, Mal,' said Ellie.

Amanda watched bewitchingly as he looked into Ellie's eyes, grabbed a hold of her hand and rose to his feet. Upon realising she had never before seen the two youngsters together, Amanda wondered if his reluctance to communicate was related to Ellie's imprisonment. In any case, the breakthrough couldn't have come at a better time.

Amanda led the children outside, checking the land nervously for Christian, but he was nowhere to be seen. She moved quickly towards Walter's car and unlocked it, feeling a great sense of achievement as the children climbed in. This was the story she had always craved. It was the story that would finally help her deal with her past. She started the engine, the wheels span eagerly as she left the car park at speed and as she drove down the hill, she saw Arthur standing there, unlocking the gate as she approached. As he pulled it open, Amanda looked out to the land beyond the Prince Care Home. It was a vision of beauty that represented success and relief.

We made it! She thought, in what was, without doubt, the greatest moment of her life.

Bang!

Bang!

From the top of the hill, Christian fired his shotgun. This time, however, the target was not the beast but the wheels of Walter's car. Such was the speed at which Amanda drove, she veered off course and crashed straight into the cumbersome base of a tree. Smoke poured out of the engine, which chugged along rather falteringly. It took a moment for the children to get their bearings as they recovered somewhat hazily from the impact. They looked over their collective cuts and bruises, but the superficial pain couldn't compare to what they felt when they saw Amanda slumped forward on the dashboard.

'Amanda?' asked Ellie, somewhat timidly, as she pulled at the woman's shoulder.

Amanda's eyes were open, but she didn't move. A heavy stream of blood poured down her face and dripped onto the floor of the car. Instantly, upon impact, Amanda had been taken, ripped away from the world without so much as a final word.

The future that she dreamed of was over.

The life that grew inside of her was gone.

The story that she seemed so destined to tell would never be heard.

*

Christian marched down the hill and looked towards Arthur in disappointment.

'Get these kids back inside *now*!' he asserted.

Terrified, Arthur immediately did as instructed, feeling every bit as sad as the crestfallen children who bawled as he led them back towards the house.

From the periphery, Elijah limped gingerly as he tended to the gunshot wound in his abdomen. He winced in pain as he touched it. He was alive but wished he wasn't. The injury rendered him useless as he watched Christian pull Amanda's body from the car and position it strategically onto the ground, using the claw from his necklace to tear through her skin as though she had been savagely attacked by a rabid animal. Christian then re-entered the house, where Walter had passed, and used the claw to similar effect as he staged a mini-massacre. Finally, he walked over to Karen. The claw would not be needed on her as Elijah had held nothing back. When confronted by such a horrific sight, most people would instinctively look away, but Christian stood silently fascinated by each violent detail. All of a sudden, his concentration was disrupted as her hand twitched. Christian had often seen a dead body move due to misfiring nerves and as he monitored her keenly, the twitching soon stopped. Incredibly, though, her eyes flickered open and she started gasping for breath.

Against all the odds, she was still alive.

*

Tony sat nervously at his desk. The sickly feeling he had experienced over the most testing five days of his life was getting worse. Every time the door clicked open on the office floor he would look up expecting to see Amanda and then glare at whoever was stood in her place.

A thousand times he had played out what to say when she finally arrived, though he felt certain when the time finally came, his mind would go blank and he would only think to say 'I love you.'

As the hours passed, Tony felt his sanity slipping away, and when it reached seven o'clock in the evening, he decided that enough was enough. Their relationship might have been on the ropes and she may very well have been chasing a story, but never did she fail to keep to a schedule without calling with an update.

Something was wrong.

He knew this for certain and so he wrote a note, grabbed his coat and picked up his car keys, placing the message on the desk before finally leaving the office.

Amanda,
Forgive me if I'm overreacting but as I haven't heard from you, I can't help but worry. I'm driving down to Devon to check you're okay. I will stop to call the office every hour in the event that I miss you in passing, so if you arrive to this note, just sit tight.
I love you,
Tx

*

Blue and red lights flashed over the Prince Care Home where paramedics and police officers swarmed around the land like flies, inspecting the bodies and recording evidence. Christian delivered his well thought-out verdict to an officer who took his statement with interest and, as the telephone rang, only Arthur remained to take the call.

'H-hello?' he said, awkwardly.

'Arthur?' replied the woman, pleasantly surprised to hear his voice.

'Lydia!' he said, joyfully, breaking into an immediate grin.

'They're letting me out, Arthur,' she revealed. 'You'll be seeing me very soon.'

For all of Christian's planning, there were three details that he knew nothing about: that his wife would be returning home with an agenda in direct conflict with his, that Amanda's soon-to-be vengeful partner was on his way to Exmoor and that somewhere, hidden beneath the floorboards of the house, lay the evidence that threatened to expose the family's most villainous of secrets.

THE END

Epilogue

LYDIA HAD EXPERIENCED THE FEELING several times before. That of *nearly* finding happiness; *almost* tasting success, but it was as though some mystical force was stalking her, tasked with keeping all good things just beyond her grasp for sins committed in a previous life.

Stepping outside of the asylum was indeed peculiar. If she were to hold a conversation with somebody in the outside world, provided she didn't mention the tragedy that plagued her past or the vivid nightmares that made her so afraid to sleep, they would probably assume she was an ordinary person. Some might even wish to be friends.

Normality – the sense of feeling normal – was a luxury she had not been afforded for a very long time, yet there she was, outdoors and without a warden to dissect her every move. Not for twelve years had she been so independent, although she was not yet completely free from the gaze of the chief warden, who she noticed peering out from his office window above the main entrance, allowing him to judge those who left and entered.

Having skillfully maneuvered a situation where she could blackmail him for her freedom, she felt certain she had not seen the last of him. He was a deeply flawed human being, a man with many perversions and an inner sense of grandeur that Lydia's recent victory would undoubtedly have threatened, but his retaliation would not come today. That wasn't how he played things. Like her, he was both a planner and a patient observer. Without any doubt, he would take his time, as he always did with the women in his facility.

Lydia walked to the end of the car park, then the road, then the many fields around her. It started to drizzle but she didn't mind. To be outside and in charge of her own destiny was strangely empowering and, on that day, there would not have been a soul on earth happier to get wet and meander.

Eventually, she came to a quaint village where everybody's lives seemed so enviably simple. They held conversations that weren't rushed and took time to say "hello" to all of those around them, including her.

'Good morning,' she replied, shyly, feeling liberated by each brief exchange.

She stumbled upon a café that invited her in with its warmth and sat patiently at a table until a waitress passed by.

'Can I get you anything, my love?'

'I have four pounds-sixty. What can I get with that?' she asked, stacking her coins on the table and pushing them forward as though they were chips in a casino.

The waitress monitored her closely.

Damn it! Though Lydia, angry that she had lost the normalcy tag so quickly.

'I can get you the works if you're hungry?'

'I need a taxi, too. Perhaps I'll just have a coffee.'

'Okaaaaay. White? Sugar?' asked the waitress, a pencil hovering above her small notepad.

'Yes. Please.'

The waitress stalled.

'One? Two?'

'Oh! Just the one, please,' confirmed Lydia, blushing as the waitress sighed and walked away.

Lydia decided it was okay. The next person she spoke to would think she was normal for much longer. She sat and enjoyed her coffee, along with the two she ordered after that. It was extraordinary how much the mind wandered when a person wasn't locked in a dark and dingy room, although she didn't understand why she still felt like a prisoner, as though her ankles were bound by heavy chains that would let her travel no further.

For twelve long years she had waited for the opportunity to return to the home and exact revenge on the people who showed her only abandonment when they were supposed to show love and who turned their backs on her when she needed them most. They left her to rot in the hands of people who should never have been trusted to care for those with such delicate conditions. Now that she was free, though, she doubted if she had the strength to overcome them. Imagining how she would deal with them whilst scorned was one thing, but physically implementing her ideas was quite another.

I'm pathetic!

I'm weak!

What am I going to do?

Lydia looked around, searchingly, for no reason other than the fact she was at a complete loss. On the table directly across from her was an old man who sat alone as he read a newspaper. As he focused on the sports updates, the front page was clear for all to see.

Exmoor beast claims life of journalist!

Suddenly, all of Lydia's reservations disappeared. How dare they blame her son for their atrocities! How dare they seek sympathy when they are such malicious, calculated liars! *They* were the guilty ones, and everybody in the home was at their mercy. No matter how Lydia figured it, there was only one person who knew or cared enough to fight for change and ensure the children were no longer subject to the same level of neglect she had been. It would take everything she had, but it was her duty.

'Another coffee, dear?' asked the waitress.

'Actually, I wondered if you could call me that taxi?'

'Sure! Where you headed?'

Lydia looked back to the picture on the paper.

'I'm going home,' she uttered, with a level of conviction that seemed to take the waitress by surprise. 'I'm going to see my boy.'

Afterword

The Moors is a hugely important project to me. Firstly, because it is the first thing I ever wrote outside of school. I didn't have to do this piece of work, but there I was as a young man, using my free time to do it anyway. The freedom I felt when creating this new world was like nothing else I had experienced. It was invigorating, and suddenly the daft idea I had about becoming a writer seemed a lot less ridiculous.

Secondly, and maybe more profoundly, I was writing about something I knew. This, as they say, is what all writers should do, but you don't necessarily listen to such advice during your teens. After more than a decade of experimental writing, though, it is this very story I have returned to when selecting which piece of work should be marked as my first commercial novel. How funny that the mystical heritage of Devon – the place where I grew up and was so desperate to get away from – has become so integral to my learning and understanding of the world.

The Moors embraces horror – something I have always been fascinated by. That the story is set in the seventies is largely because this, in my opinion, was the golden age of the genre. Films such as *The Texas Chainsaw Massacre* and *The Wicker Man* made for such uncomfortable yet mesmerising viewing, and these films never quite left me.

In fact, it was whilst delivering bouncy castles during the summer of 1998 that the idea of *The Moors* was born. By day, the house I had visited was a picture of tranquillity, set in the middle of Exmoor on the grounds of a large, wealthy home. However, when I returned to collect the castle that night, the mood was very different. Sinister shadows replaced areas where the sun had earlier thrived and an eerie silence stalked the land around me. It got me thinking "If anything bad were to happen to me now, I'd be completely alone."

As the trees danced in the breeze and alien sounds were exaggerated in my mind, the way I felt combined with the stories

I'd been told about the mysterious Exmoor beast during my youth, and suddenly an inescapable idea began to grow.

I am not a fan of modern slasher flicks or teenage horror books. In fact, what people consider to be a "horror" these days do not compare to the more psychological stories I eagerly consumed during my younger years; stories that have long lived in my mind. To me, that is the trick of a good horror – making something that gets under a person's skin and makes them believe the concept is feasible; that it could actually happen to them; that it could be real.

The Moors poured out of me because it is the type of story I myself would love to read, and so my hope is you will enjoy reading the book every bit as much as I enjoyed making it. If you do then please take a moment to review it on Amazon, or post a more extensive review on Goodreads. It can't be stressed enough how much these contributions help.

About the Author

JODY MEDLAND is an award-winning writer who has worked successfully across the advertising, education, film, gaming, literary and television industries.

His debut feature film, *The Adored*, was released in the States in 2013 and has since enjoyed worldwide distribution, including territories such as the UK, Germany, Poland and Uganda. It won Best Film at the Durban Film Festival in South Africa and earned three official selections in Wales, Germany and the US.

Jody is deeply passionate about his literary work and from 2011-2012 he produced and published ten short story books, titled *The Emerging Light Series* – a project that encouraged new writers to create and submit short stories.

It is the ability to wield strong, original concepts that Jody is renowned for among his peers and he is a great fan of dramas, thrillers and mystical stories, which are his genres of choice when writing.